I0682011

COST OF
FREEDOM

KATHERINE
ZARTMAN

Lavender Moon Publishing

Cost of Freedom
All Rights Reserved.
Copyright © 2020 Katherine Zartman
v3.0

This is a work of fiction. Names, characters, businesses,
places, events, locales, and incidents are either the products
of the author's imagination or used in a fictitious manner. Any
resemblance to actual persons, living or dead, or actual events
is purely coincidental.

The opinions expressed in this manuscript are solely the
opinions of the author and do not represent the opinions or
thoughts of the publisher. The author has represented and
warranted full ownership and/or legal right to publish all the
materials in this book.

This book may not be reproduced, transmitted, or stored in
whole or in part by any means, including graphic, electronic,
or mechanical without the express written consent of the publisher except in the case of brief quotations embodied in critical articles and reviews.

Lavender Moon Publishing

ISBN: 978-0-578-23052-8

Cover Photo © 2020 www.gettyiages.com. All rights reserved
- used with permission.

PRINTED IN THE UNITED STATES OF AMERICA

CHAPTER ONE

I pull into the crowded parking lot and wonder who will be missing today. My work at this busy VA hospital is both rewarding and heartbreaking. Assigned now to the newly formed hospice unit, death row with no chance of appeal, Mike the guard greets me and unlocks the door to the day's horrors. We talk briefly, and he coughs. "Arlene, we lost Ted last night." Oh, no. I close my eyes and see Ted, rugged, bearded, and no legs. A World War II vet suffering from heart failure. I have spent many hours listening to the dark memories of this brave man on the battlefields of Germany. A tank commander proud of his service and feeling a deep desire to spend his last days at home with his wife of forty years. Most veterans here love to talk about their war encounters, and it serves as a distraction while we take care of their needs. "Fuck, Mike, I will miss him." One of the first lessons I learned working for the VA is the language and dialect of its inhabitants. The unique use of the F-word frequently screamed during a painful or difficult procedure. A vent of frustration from the "Why me?" aura that surrounds them. It is so much a part of their language, and I am no longer furtive to use it. I do not flinch or admonish them when I hear it; sometimes, in fact, it is shouted or screamed delivering lunch trays or cleaning wounds. Fuck yes, vets are a rowdy bunch. I push my thoughts and make my way into the unit.

Another day, the smell already disturbing my nostrils. You can never get away from the ammonia, the raw scent in the wards. I stop and say hello to Harry, Ted's roommate, and give him a hug. He needs a diaper change, I observe, and I pull on gloves to facilitate my first change of the day. Harry is silent but lifts his hips as I release the tabs that hold the diaper in place. He rolls to the side and grabs a handrail, so I can pull the diaper from underneath him. Love it when the patient knows the routine, and I don't have to call an orderly. I clean him up and wipe the tears spilling from his sad eyes. I bend and kiss his forehead and whisper, "I know, Harry—I will miss him too."

I pull the blanket over him and slowly walk to the nurses' station to see the schedule for the day. Dressing changes, showers, outside breaks, and I am to go to Dr. Cross's office for a consult. A busy day, and I wonder what Dr. Cross wants to talk to me about. I don't think I've done anything wrong, so what am I in for?

I look at the schedule again and head down to Taylor's for his shower. Taylor suffers from advanced renal disease and needs a shower before his appointment in dialysis. He winks at me and grunts when I roll his wheelchair to the bedside and pull the transfer board to help him into the chair. He starts to pull his gown off, and I tell him, "Not yet—let me get the shower warm first." He grunts again and relaxes as I adjust the water temperature and arrange the shampoo and body wash on the lower shelf. I again set the transfer board and settle him onto the shower seat. Soaped, cleaned, a quick shave, and Taylor is ready to go. I pat his shoulder once a clean gown is on him, and he again grunts, pleased to be warm and clean. A stroke several months ago has taken his voice, and soon disease will take his life. I leave the door open, and with a quick look down the hall, I see the crew coming to take him to dialysis.

Two doors down I enter Aaron's room and ask him, "How was breakfast?"

"Fucking cold eggs again and no jelly for the toast. Can't they ever get it right?"

I smile at him and pull the supply cart over to the bed. "Swing your legs over here so I can change your dressings." Aaron huffs and yells, "I don't have fucking legs anymore to swing!" I help him to the side of the bed and ask him his pain level.

"Fucking ten! Just get on with it."

I pull bandages, gauze, and antibiotic medication from the supply cart, put on gloves, and start to carefully remove the bandage from both leg amputations. Aaron was lucky that the gangrene which precipitated the amputations was removed before it got above his knees. Once healed, if he's still alive, he will have much better movement with knees intact for the prosthetic limbs. I call the nurses' station—Aaron needs pain medication.

I just need to take Fred for an outside break and then head to Dr. Cross's office before lunch. I walk briskly down the hall and greet Fred, already waiting by the locked exit door. It is a bit cool, so I return to his room and collect his robe, placing it around his shoulders and tucking it down his sides. "Nice robe, Fred. Are you warm enough?"

"Yeah. My daughter brought it for me, and we had a great visit."

"You're lucky, Fred. She is a beautiful girl, and she loves her daddy."

He nods, and I signal Mike to come unlock the door to the patio, and soon Fred is outside enjoying the clear sky and early morning sun. He is animated and tells me about his daughter's visit. We fall quiet, and I look at my watch. I ring for Mike to open the door and return Fred to his room. I pat his hand and tell him I'll come by tomorrow with some cookies, and he smiles, closing his eyes for a nap.

CHAPTER TWO

I venture to the restroom and check my appearance before heading to Dr. Cross's office at the main hospital. I knock on his door and peek around the frame.

"Hi, Arlene, how are you?"

"I'm great, sir. What can I do for you?"

"I have a proposition for you. I've been hearing good things from patients and staff about you working in the hospice unit. You seem to have a closeness and the ability to relate to the veterans."

"Yes, sir. I am a vet myself, as you know, and my dad was an air force colonel. I know the military, and I love hearing the war stories—each different but proudly told. I am also a war buff, love the old movies and the histories in each of them; World War II is my favorite. So, what is your proposition, sir?"

Dr. Cross leans back in his chair and says, "Wonderful."

I smile and say, "What do you need?"

"Well, as you know, I am the head shrink here, and I have a group of PTSD patients who could use another voice in our sessions. I would like you to attend a few and see if you can tolerate the environment. It can be violent and tearful, but these men are suffering, and I think you could help displace some of their anxiety. I don't expect an answer until you have met the group and experienced a few sessions."

"Yes, sir, I think I could help. Are any of them prone to violence?"

"Of course, but we have immediate help available, should we need it. Our first session will be Wednesday. I'll make the arrangements to transfer you, and you can let your patients know what is going on."

"Yes, sir. Thank you for your confidence in me; I look forward to the next challenge."

I stand, a little wobbly, and return to my unit for lunch. I speak with the girls at the nurses' station and tell them about this opportunity. They are all thrilled but agree my guys here will not be. I collect my lunch and exit to a sunny picnic table outside and go through the conversation I had with Dr. Cross. I am excited but worried. Can I help these damaged men? Will I be safe? I need to do some research before agreeing, and how do I say goodbye to my guys in hospice?

Lunch is over, and John's shower is due. I ring the door for Mike and head to John's room.

"Hey, Arlene, get me out of these clothes; I itch all over."

I laugh and glove my hands from the dispenser by the door. John—unable to exist without someone's care—has severe coronary disease and no arms. They were cruelly blown off by an IUD in Afghanistan. He is a favorite of mine, always a smile or a joke and easy to care for. I feed him, bathe him, and dress him every day.

"Do you need to use the toilet first, John, or are you good to go?"

"No. Andrea was in earlier and took care of me."

"Be good, and I'll leave you with a treat."

"Oh boy, man for a day, I can't wait!"

I reach for his hips and guide him to the edge of the bed. His fancy wheelchair can be raised, so it is easy to transfer him to the chair. Most vets are not this lucky, but John has a lot of money from stock portfolios. How am I going to tell him I'm leaving hospice? Another family member, gone overnight. I pull him to the shower and transfer him to the bench, John's expensive array of soaps, shampoos, and lotions standing guard, awaiting hands that are not his own. Once he is scrubbed down and smelling of autumn and pine, I carefully dry him and go to collect his treat. Pulling a pair of gray briefs and gray sweat pants, I return and tell John to stand. I steady him, and he dutifully raises one leg at a time for me to slip the clothes on.

"Oh, Arlene, how good you make me feel, and how great to be a man for the day." I know the comfort of wearing soft underwear and sweatpants is frowned on by the staff, but it is soothing to my vets and brings a small joy to their restless souls. I softly smack his now warmly dressed behind, and John says, "Oh, if I only I could return the favor!"

"Hush now, and I'll bring you the chocolate."

John and I have become very familiar with each other over his months in the hospice unit. As I'm breaking the chocolate onto his food tray, I remember the day he cried while I was dressing him and his soulful request to have underwear on so he could feel like a man again. The tradition has become like a holiday to this poor man and only a soft bending of the unit's rules. If it brings a few hours of joy into the lonely days, who could fault me? I give John a piece of chocolate, and he grins, now savoring the second part of his treat. I kiss his head and smile as he calls after me, "Great ass! Thanks for the treat!" I make a mental note to ask Andrea to continue the tradition with John, as it is a simple pleasure much desired and only given by me. I wink at John and tell him to behave.

Joe is waiting for a dressing change, so I make my way to his room. Obviously in pain, Joe asks for pain medication before I change the dressing. I tap and bring up his chart; there has been no medication given other than the early a.m. dose. I tell him to hold on and that I'll go get his meds and come back as soon as possible. A grim smile and a wave to go.

"Sorry. We just missed it."

"Okay. Order a vanilla milkshake for Joe and call me when you have it."

Angry, I rush back to Joe and give him his meds. I fuss with the bed and towels in the bathroom, waiting a few minutes for the pain to lessen. His face has softened, and he nods okay for me to slowly peel down the wet and soiled bandage from his middle. He has several drains left, and I empty them; the stitches look good, and the swelling is down. Stomach cancer has left Joe weak and thin. He qualified for hospice but will not survive much longer as the cancer is very aggressive. I pat his shoulder, and he closes his eyes. The pain has eased, so I finish putting clean bandages and write a short note for him. "Vanilla shake in the fridge when you wake from your nap. Remember, you have a call button, and talk with staff when you need meds—don't wait until you are uncomfortable. Enjoy your shake. I'll see you tomorrow. Arlene."

I walk back through the unit, and most are asleep. Fred is watching his soap opera. He follows it every weekday and wants someone to converse with over the episode. A quiet end to the day. Now I must do some PTSD research and explore my feelings on this pressure cooker and possibly dangerous challenge.

CHAPTER THREE

My watch says 2:40—time to go to the staff lounge and meet the vets in this rotation. I am now somewhat prepared for what awaits me upstairs. My research uncovered surprising numbers of suicide, violence, and occupations subject to the rigors of PTSD. Police, firefighters, and battle-hardened veterans of every conflict. Known as battle fatigue in WWII, bomber pilots were pulled often just before a mission, catatonic and perhaps shivering with fear, prevented from the mission though desperately needed. Slow to be recognized by the medical field as a legitimate ailment and given a proper name. Much the same as "the gay disease" had claimed thousands before being recognized as AIDS.

I push my thoughts aside and open the door at the staff lounge; seven sets of eyes

12

follow me onto one of the sofas. "Good afternoon, Arlene. Join us for this session."

A few smiles, and two patients jump to their feet, but most are unhappy at my intrusion. Dr. Cross explains why I am here and asks for a welcome.

"Why the fuck does she have to be in here? I won't stay if she does."

Not exactly a good start, but I relax, put a smile on my face, and scan the eyes sweeping over my position. The two who stood up say, "Fuck this, I'm leaving. Why the fuck can a woman know anything about combat?" Others shout to "shut the fuck up," and Dr. Cross asks the two disruptors to leave. I stand and ask Dr. Cross to talk with me in the hall.

We excuse ourselves, and he immediately says, "Rough start, but I expected it." I agree with him but wonder if I can be of any help.

"Yes, Arlene. Just be patient. This s a slow process, and the guys don't know or trust you yet."

We return to the lounge, and Dr. Cross introduces me, giving the four remaining vets a short summary of my experience. A few smiles return, along with a few admiring looks.

Bill, the first to be introduced. A helicopter

pilot maimed in a crash while picking up wounded at an LZ, Vietnam, 1969. We nod at each other and smile. Mike, a mechanic for the motor pool, no physical injuries, Iraq. Ryan, burns from napalm under friendly fire, Vietnam, 1971. And finally, Lars. Norwegian born, blond, right leg and left hand missing. Shrapnel wound to the neck, gunner on a Huey, Vietnam, 1970.

"Well, gentlemen, give her a chance, and she will return the trust." Bill smiles and nods his head, Mike turns his head, Ryan pulls his shirt over his face, and Lars smiles and shifts in his seat. I sit down by each of them and spend a few moments learning about their current status: married, single, kids, employed, year of their diagnosis, known triggers of the disease.

Bill is open and answers my questions as a student would in school. Mike is hesitant and seems confused. Ryan refuses any conversation and continues to hide behind his shirt. Lars is forthcoming: single, no kids, looking forward to many talks in the future.

It is 17:00 ; I stand and squeeze a shoulder of each. "See you next session."

Dr. Cross and I talk softly in the hall, and he tells me that he won't bring back the two who left the session. Too much animosity against a woman, not productive to progress with the four others. I agree and tell him I look forward to one more time with each. I'm a bit concerned about Ryan, the napalm victim. Dr. Cross tells me, "Yes, he is going to be a hard case. Divorced after he was burned; his wife could not cope. Many surgeries, grafts, and a boatload of self-loathing. Stay positive."

CHAPTER FOUR

I stop the car as I'm leaving the parking lot. The sign welcoming visitors' flashes on and off; the price of freedom can be seen here. Yes, it is not just seen—it is inhaled in every corner. After a restless night, I return to the hospice unit and tearfully say goodbye to my buddies there. Joe, the stomach cancer victim, has lost his battle due to heart failure. John is beside himself when I tell him I'm leaving. Tears fall, and he begs me to stay. "Arlene, please." I wipe away the tears as he cannot, and I promise I will visit often. God, how do I cope with this? These men are family, and I am so aware of the many intimate moments they have been forced to share with me because of handicaps. I brood in the car on the way home and visualize their faces and injuries, and I ask that they be blessed and hope they do not suffer for my care lost to them.

John will be the most sensitive and does not adjust well to change. I will make sure to visit him every week. I open a bottle of white wine when I reach home and spend the evening's sorrows watching the volume disappear.

As I open the door for our next PTSD session, all four are talking softly together and shout, "Welcome back, Arlene!" Dr. Cross winks and gestures for me to sit. Bill comes over and pats my knee. "Ready for interrogation." Bill is divorced; the noise of a helicopter or sight of one triggers heated anger in him.

"I forced my wife to divorce me by screaming at her and her family. I constantly, as you can see, wring my damaged hands together." He is also missing his left foot, the prosthetic tucked under the sofa, out of view.

"Tell me about your wife. Why did you take your anger out on her?"

"I don't know for sure, but her father was a helicopter pilot for the evening news, and I took out my anger on her. There is always a reason and never a solution, Arlene."

"We can work on this—trust me."

I thank Bill for his honestly and move over next to Mike—no physical injuries but a damaged outlook at the world. He cannot be around transportation of any kind; hard to do in this world. He stammers, "I don't like cars or trucks."

"We will work on this. Not even Corvettes?"

He smiles and blinks at me.

I walk across the room and sit next to Ryan. I place my hand over his and tell him we are going to be friends. He looks at me and then quickly pulls his hand from under mine.

"Look at me, Ryan."

"I can't, and you shouldn't look at me; I'm a fucking nightmare."

"I've seen worse, and you speak well for such damaged vocal cords."

"Yeah, can I sing you the national fucking anthem?"

I pat his hand again and tell him, "We are going to be friends, anyway."

I glance over at Lars and mouth, "You're next." He smiles and pats the sofa next to him on his right side, the left missing a hand, of course. I sit where he indicates, and he immediately closes his long fingers over mine and smiles broadly. "I want to know you really well, Arlene, so don't be afraid of my injuries."

"Lars, I have seen much worse, and you are still a beautiful, strong, Norwegian blond. Tall, a relic of the Vikings."

His whole face lights up, and he pulls my

hand to his lips. A soft kiss, and I tell him I enjoyed our little talk, but I need to hear more. Dr. Cross signals that it is 17:00. Another session done.

CHAPTER FIVE

D r. Cross and I talk briefly in the hall. "I'm not sure I can help, or if I give the wrong advice, if I could cause more damage."

"Not at all. I watch you, and I watch their reactions. You are doing great; just keep it up. Even Ryan responded to you. It is so rare so keep it up, Arlene, and I'll see you at the end of the week."

I stop by hospice to see John, but he isn't there, so I leave a note for him. "Sorry I missed you; hope you are well and happy and still getting treats. You can always have Andrea write a letter for you—my address is on the back. See you soon. Fondly, Arlene."

I stop at the nurses' station to find out how John is doing. "Not well. His cardiac numbers are dropping."

"Just tell him I left a note and rubbed his pillow; he missed a kiss on his forehead."

"You are too much, Arlene. Everybody misses you." I pull a twenty from my wallet and tell Andrea to order an extra-large pizza for the group. "Tell them, 'Arlene misses you.'"

Bill is animated at the next session and says he is learning to live with the sound of choppers except the ones flying into the VA with emergency patients, stateside war. A brief call with his ex-wife made him happy. "Wonderful news, Bill. Heal thyself."

Mike has a small group of Hot Wheels arranged on the table in front of him. He picks up a Corvette and splays his hand, showing the assortment of tractors, dump trucks, and other farm vehicles—all noticeably non-military transport. Progress so fast? Maybe I should go back to school and finish a degree in psychology.

Ryan has a slight smile and leans into me as I sit beside him. "What is it, Ryan? It is only skin deep; you are still unscarred underneath. Call your sister and have her visit. She is family and wants her big brother's wisdom and advice." Ryan pulls back, smiles, and nods his head rather slowly.

Lars is again anxious for our talk; he covers my hand again as I take a seat on his right side. "I missed you, Arlene."

"I missed my Viking too. Tell me about the Huey, why it was so easily shot down."

Lars hesitates and then slowly relates the lack of weaponry on the chopper. Only his M60 as a weapon. "The NVA had several missiles they could launch faster than we could lift off an LZ because we were loading wounded under fire. I killed many, and there was so much blood on the floor when we unloaded the wounded. I always thought I would get it leaning out the open side, and one day, I did."

CHAPTER SIX

Lars says, "Can we go out to dinner?"
"Whoa! Brazen, but not a bad idea. I will talk to Dr. Cross."

He brings my hand again to his mouth and softly kisses it. A Viking with a much softer demeanor. He appeals to me in a visceral way. Blond, handsome—I don't see the loss of his right leg and left hand. There are more important visuals to distract me.

Dr. Cross is again happy to see his team progress. He is not sure dinner with Lars is appropriate, but "amputees have few chances to date, and you are a strong woman, up to a challenge. Do as you wish."

I will let it simmer for now. It's just too new; however, it has been a few years since my last date, and I do feel a surge of excitement for one. My buddies in hospice are a definite no as they are all under a death sentence and need no emotional complications. Speaking of which, I need to check on John.

I am distressed when I see a white sheet of paper on his door; I know it is a DNR requested by John. "Do not resuscitate; let me go, no heroics, CPR, or any other attempts to keep me alive." I peek around the door, and John is sleeping. Checking his pulse at his neck, I frown when I can just barely discern the count. I tuck his blanket firmly around him all the way up to his chin, just the way he likes it since he is unable to do it himself. I softly kiss him on the forehead, and he mumbles something I don't understand. Tears come quickly, and I softly whisper, "Sleep well, John."

I stop and speak with Andrea. "The cardiologist was with him earlier in the day. Unresponsive; he probably won't make it to the morning."

The tears involuntarily begin again, and I feel a tightness in my chest. Goodbye, sweet John; your service has ended, and I will miss you. Hospice. Death row with no hope of an appeal. A softer way to die, the same bitter end unknown in advance by the inmate.

Enough morbid thoughts. I'll just think of his often-stupid jokes and his gratitude when

Cost of Freedom

I pulled underwear on him. So strange to be so happy with his soft, expensive underwear. John had no family, but I know he talked often with his lawyer and had made final arrangements. Life is full of little chips at your heart, carving it with no sense of art. Time for bed, a cup of hot chocolate, and much-needed sleep for my restless mind. Goodnight, John.

CHAPTER SEVEN

I arrive early to the PTSD group and watch their slow arrival. Bill is animated; Mike is silent and clutches his backpack with his now precious small vehicles. Ryan rubs his face and itches the area where his ears were before the napalm. Lars sports a shy smile and nods his head rapidly up and down. How quickly I can read the group temperature. I move to talk to Bill, and he signals me to see Lars first. "He has a secret he wants you to hear; driving us crazy because he won't tell us anything."

The now-familiar fingers close over my hand, and he whispers, "Dr. Cross talked to me and said I could take you to dinner but not to tell the other guys; it would upset them." I tell him, "Yes it would hurt their ego because I chose you over them, and Ryan could be dangerous. I'm off Friday, so I will pick you up. What would you like to eat for dinner?"

"No hesitation, Red Lobster. I'm Norwegian, love seafood!"

"I can fit your wheelchair in the car."

He shakes his head. "No prosthesis; it hurts the stump. I'll use my crutches."

"Are you able to handle a few stairs and a crowded restaurant?"

"I will lean on you if I can't. I'm so excited, Arlene. Remember: not a word to the other guys."

Ryan stands and says, "Taking long enough, Lars? She needs to talk to all of us." Sensing some anger, I turn and pat Ryan's shoulder. "How are you this week?"

"I itch like hell where my ears were."

I tell him to talk to a PA as they can order several anti-itch creams for the discomfort. "Now, tell me how you came into contact with napalm from our troops."

"Our unit was being overrun, and the captain ordered an air strike. Six minutes later the jets arrived and sprayed the hillside with napalm. It came too close, and I ran out to call them off the run. My mistake. I was immediately engulfed until a few buddies knocked me down, screaming to roll around. Unimaginable pain. They kept throwing water on me, which made my uniform stick to me, which made the debridement later at the hospital even more painful. I still feel the pain when I look at the results in a mirror or hear a jet."

"Oh, Ryan, the pain and tragedy of war cannot be predicted or halted—just accepted, as you almost have. As you know, I see beyond the ravaged skin and recognize the courage it takes you to overcome the horror of your lot in life. Thank you for talking to me. It always helps."

I hear Mike vocalizing, crashing his tractor into haybales, and I tell him sharply to stop. "Farming equipment provides you with food. Get your Corvette and tell me the engine size. As I remember, the early ones had a 256, frequently punched out to a 302. Am I right, Mike?"

He scratches his head and opens his phone to research the 'Vette. Bill is squirming in his seat and can contain his excitement no more. "My sister is coming for a visit, and I can stay with them for a weekend. They live in the country and have horses and dogs. I can't wait."

I pinch his shoulders and tell him, "Yes, family can always overlook damage done and heal the emotional wounds. Remember that." Happy again, Dr. Cross says he needs to adjust his training to include empathy from attractive women. I'm sure I blush, and I think again about finishing a second college degree. Yeah, right, at my age?

CHAPTER EIGHT

Wednesday comes, and I am subdued after confirming John had passed the same day that I saw him. Another cost of freedom to join the ranks of white crosses dotting our cemeteries. I force a smile when I enter the lounge of my PTSD group. Everyone is smiling—Lars with a face-splitting grin. We talk briefly and catch up on good news. Lars whispers, "I'm about to combust with excitement; are you?" I hush him and tell him, "Behave. We'll see." We whisper arrangements, and later I go shopping for a new outfit. Excitement and thoughts of what will happen Friday motivate me beyond my depressed mood earlier.

Friday comes, and I pick up Lars in front of the VA. I have made reservations at Red Lobster, always a busy place. Lars is a little off-balance with his single crutch and shoves his left forearm into his jacket pocket. He looks handsome in his tweed jacket and washed jeans. I'm sure I'm the only one to know there is no leg under his right pant leg. His crutch catches on a transition strip to the dining area. I steady him by putting my arm around his waist. Surprised, he leans over and kisses my cheek. "Yeah, this is going to be a fun night."

Lars orders shrimp and lobster, a loaded baked potato, and salad. I settle for steak and lobster, knowing I will eat too many biscuits. We talk about Norway as he is a native of the country and I had visited several times when Dad was stationed in Germany, contributing to the dramatic healing and rebuilding for the German people. Lars asks for the check and tells me he has saved every paycheck since there is no cost at the VA. I squeeze his hand and tell him he is very lucky. He says, "We should go; now what?"

I respond, "I thought we could go to my place and get naked." Lars laughs and says, "Just what I want too."

Only a few miles to my house, and Lars is so anxious, it's infectious. He looks around the house and loves my art studio and library. Spying the fireplace, he asks to start a fire.

"Yes, just make sure the damper is open." I tell him I'll open some wine and ask if he would like a glass. "Yes, I need courage."

I respond, "Don't worry—I won't hurt you." He laughs and pulls me to him, slightly off-balance again. He sports a few charcoal marks from the fireplace and downs the wine. "More, please."

Gulping a second glass, he pulls me to him and runs his only hand down my front, stopping at my breasts and asking if it's okay. I give him a soft kiss, tousle his hair, and hand him the crutch. "Follow me to my bedroom."

He hesitates just a beat and says, "I haven't done this since before Vietnam. I may be a little clumsy."

I confess, "It has been many years for me too. We'll manage."

He stops in front of the bed, and I turn, unzip his jeans, and pull them off, along with his briefs. He is embarrassed when his stump is exposed. I reassure him that as a nurse at the VA, I have seen everything possible. He relaxes and drops the crutch to the floor. I pull my shirt and camisole off and join him on the bed. His erection is generous and surrounded by more blond hair. I bend down and take him in my mouth; he pulls back and says, "No, I

Cost of Freedom

won't last if you do this." I back off, and he is a
bit clumsy trying to caress my breasts. His right
hand is perfectly at home, but his left arm has
no hand, so the stump kind of slides around.
"Sorry, I need to relearn how to do this."

"Let me solve your problem, Lars—use
your mouth instead." He follows my lead and
grunts with pleasure. I know he will have
trouble getting on top of me, so I push him
on his back and position myself over him. "I
won't last long," he murmurs, and I tell him,
"We have all night." He relaxes, and I kiss him
deeply while I surreptitiously guide him into
me. He groans, and I establish a slow but re-
lentless rhythm for us. He still shows signs of
being off-balance, so I put my arm around his
right hip to help his thrusts. His breathing becomes ragged, and mine escalates as well. He
shouts as he comes and collapses like a rag
doll. He says, "Now it is your turn."

I pry myself from his body and lie down
on his right side. He kisses me, sucks my nipples, and slides his right hand down to my
sex. It is filled with his semen, so he needs no
lubricant. I gently guide his hand, and soon he
has me panting for relief.

"Oh, Arlene, we are good together; just
give me a little time to recuperate."

"Yes. Tell me about your childhood in Norway. It is a beautiful country—I love Oslo and Copenhagen. What did your dad do, and your mom?"

"Dad worked at a lumber mill, and Mom stayed home and took care of me and my brothers."

"Sounds like a rather idyllic life, Lars."

"We came to the U.S. in 1960. I joined the marines and was taught many things. My older brother Sven was killed in 1962 in an NVA ambush."

I feel a shudder run through Lars, and I tell him to relax, and we'll talk more next time. He turns to me and says, "Next time? You mean we can do this again?"

I run my hand down to his still-flaccid cock and squeeze my acknowledgment. Since I'm already holding it, I begin to massage, running my fingertips over the tip. I feel a sudden surge through my fingers, and Lars rather awkwardly reaches for my breasts. It is his left arm—no hand, so he cannot fully grip it but bends down and nudges it until positioned for his hungry mouth. He is rising beneath me and grunts that he wants to be on top this time. I use my hands, caress his behind, and pull and adjust till he is stable and in position.

"God, Arlene, is this okay?" I squeeze my consent. "All part of my training," I murmur. Lars laughs and starts to thrust harder. I continue to apply pressure to his backside, and he soon starts to shudder his release. We both lie contented for a few moments, just looking at each other. He shifts his left leg up so he can turn and says, "I need a shower."

"Just relax. I will give you a bed bath since we don't have a chair here."

He smiles, and I rise to collect a pan, body wash, and a few hand towels. Filled with hot water and fragrant bubbles, I carefully bring the pan to my bed. Surprised that I'm not using antibacterial wipes, he says, "Yeah, I like this." I clean his face and neck, shoulders, and armpits and slowly circle his chest sprinkled with curly blond hair. I continue my downward journey and gently remove any residue from our union. I dry him and return to the bathroom for new hot water. Lars is really liking this bath. I soap up the washcloth and bend to his right leg. Lars bolts upright and says, "No, don't."

"I've seen thousands of stumps." I push him back down and continue. He grimaces as I clean the leg at the end of his stump. Noticing his discomfort, I ask if he feels pain. He nods, and I take a closer inspection. The flap used by the surgeon who amputated his leg is flat, moveable, and shows some indentation from the sawed-off bones. I tell Lars, "I think you should see Dr. Todd. I think you could use a revision surgery on the stump."

Lars looks at me, confused, and I explain. "There isn't enough padding, and the bones have a rough edge to them." He closes his eyes and says, "No, I've had enough surgery." I encourage him again and make a note to talk with Dr. Todd. I clean his other leg and then warm some oil in my hands, rubbing it into his body. He grunts his approval and raises his hips. "Take me again." I comply, and we are both sated and relaxed. Sleep comes quickly, and all too soon, the morning sun is invading the bedroom from the skylight above. Lars opens his eyes and reaches for a hand grip on the bed. There isn't one on my bed, only on his hospital bed. "I need to pee; can you help me get up?"

"Yes, of course," and I snake my arm under his right shoulder and pull him upright to the side of the bed. I retrieve his crutch and help him to stand and regain his balance. I hold onto him, and he stumbles a bit on the bathroom rug. I kick it out of the way, and he grabs the toilet seat, lifts it, and urinates. "Good morning."

I help him dress, and he follows me through the art studio, then detours to the library. "More of your wonderful paintings, and just look at your books. I'm impressed."

"I'm impressed with you, Lars. I enjoyed last night and want to know much more about you."

He pulls a photo from the bookcase and peers at it closely. I whisper, "That is me and my three children." He nods and says, "We have so much to talk about."

"We have time, but now, it is time for breakfast."

CHAPTER NINE

I drive us to a local breakfast spot, and we order omelets with fruit and toast on the side. I watch how he handles utensils, and we talk about our evening. I tell him that soon he will be discharged from the hospital and placed on outpatient status. His face shows some fear, and I reassure him that he is ready.

"Maybe, but what will I do? I'll need a house, car, furniture—too much to think about."

"Not to worry, Lars. I will help you with all of the details."

Our omelets arrive, and we grow silent, food to start our day.

Lars skirts his fingers over mine, and he says, "I think I'm falling for you, Arlene." I smile, squeeze his hand, and say, "I have strong feelings for you too. We still have some obstacles to overcome: your PTSD and life in the hospital, my family, and what is left of yours."

"I still have another brother and an aunt and uncle in Norway." We kiss, and he places his right arm around me for support.

I stop and pick up my mail before returning Lars to the hospital. I riffle through the envelopes and see a familiar name on a return address. I don't recall who it is, so I rip open the envelope to find a typed letter addressed to me from a legal firm. They wish to see me regarding the estate of John Newberry. Oh, John, even dead, you make me picture your damaged self. And the tears begin to fall. Lars is alarmed. "What's wrong, Arlene?"

I tell him, "John was a long-term hospice patient of mine, and he died last week."

"What did he die of, Arlene?"

"The poor man lost both hands and had crippling heart disease. I was close to him, and he loved me, though he was never able to tell me." Poor, poor John, I do miss seeing you. "He was heartbroken when Dr. Cross transferred me from hospice to the PTSD rotation."

Lars holds up his left arm and says, "You didn't move far."

I kiss the stump where his hand once was and wipe my tears away. "Come, I'll take you to the hospital. I have a few things to take care of."

After I drop off Lars, I return home and call the number on the letter; they would like to see me today, if possible. "I can come by at 2:00, if that is okay?"

"Great. We look forward to seeing you." I spend a few hours going through the mail and then look up the address to the law office. Yeah, I know where that is: upper floor in the bank building. I arrive at the firm and nervously enter the elevator, selecting the sixth floor. The prestigious double oak doors hold an etched glass plate naming the partners, and I push open the doors, butterflies in my belly. I sit as instructed and wait for the news. An older, well-dressed man opens a side door, carrying a stack of papers. "Arlene, welcome. John told me you were beautiful. I agree."

"So, what is this about?"

"Well, let me read you a portion of John's will." The butterflies are now dancing a salsa as the lawyer clears his throat and starts to read.

"I hereby bequeath to my beloved Arlene the sum of $20,000. Arlene, you knew me so intimately, but not in the way I wanted. Remember our treat days, so special to me—a man again, but with no hands to hold you. With this money, I hope you will remember me and feel like I just gave you a hug."

Tears fall, and the lawyer offers a box of Kleenex. "John, John, such a gentle soul. I will never forget you." The lawyer pulls a check from the stack of papers, hands it to me, and I stumble out of the palatial office. I lean against the elevator wall and stare at the check. Walking quickly to the car, I sit and lower my head to the steering wheel and cry. Stinging, warm tears turn to sobs, and I drive to the hospital to see Dr. Cross.

"Arlene, what's wrong? I can see you've been crying. Is it Lars?"

I shake my head and show him the check. He looks at it and then at me. "What? Tell me."

I tell him about John, my hospice patient, his death, and ask his advice.

"Oh, Arlene, that check is hard evidence of why I chose you for our group. You must make up your own mind. You do realize that you become their hands and legs, a gift to restore normalcy, and a beautiful woman who tends to them so intimately at times."

CHAPTER TEN

I hug Dr. Cross and go in search of Lars. I am told he is in the rehab gym but no other appointments for the day. I take the elevator up to the gym and see Lars, butterflies again dancing. He is sweating profusely, and his blond hair is dark with sweat. He sees me, pulls me to him and kisses me. "Come, will you give me a shower?"

"Yes, it will give me the opportunity to get close to you again." I help Lars into his wheelchair and go to his room two floors down.

"You're crying. Tell me, don't you like me anymore?"

"Actually, I'm beginning to think that I love you, Lars."

He smiles and pulls his shirt off. I start the shower water and ease his sweatpants down. I kiss his belly and then can't resist continuing to kiss him lower.

"So, tell me why you were crying."

"Remember John? I told you about him, one of my hospice patients, no hands, heart disease?" He nods and says, "So what is going on?" and I burst into tears again. He hugs me hard. "Arlene, what is it?"

I haltingly tell him, and he hugs me again. Sitting on the shower bench, I tell him, "Let's get you clean." I soap him and wash his hair; he lifts my shirt and kisses a breast. He definitely has a balance issue, no leg on the right, no hand on the left. I quietly explain to Lars as I help him to dress, "We are going to my house."

He becomes excited as we drive home and heads for the bedroom immediately. I pull John's check from my purse; Lars looks at it and gives me a questioning look. "John loved me and left his money to me."

"What are you going to do with it?" Lars asked.

"I have thought about this all day, and I have decided I will donate the entire amount to Wounded Warriors."

"You are too good, Arlene."

"Well, it's the best thing to do as I would always feel guilty if I did not honor his memory by selfishly using the money." I go to my dresser and pull out a leather box, open it, and hand it to Lars. "What is this?"

I tell him it is filled with mementos and memories of the vets I have taken care of. Purple Hearts, rings, watches, dog tags, letters, notes, and a few pictures. "My guys always loved the care and touch that I gave them. A nonmedical touch, a hug, a kiss on their forehead, or just a simple squeeze of their hand or toes if they didn't have a hand."

Lars holds up his handless arm and tears roll down his cheek. "I'm so glad you liked me, and your touch was so surprising to a man without a hand or a leg. You cared right away, and you are beautiful, inside and out."

"You are a very special vet to me. Get your balance, and I will show you how much."

He covers my face with kisses, and I slowly pull his sweatpants down. I kneel and take his enlarging cock into my mouth. He hugs my head with his stump and right hand, groans, and pushes his erection deeper into my throat. In and out, in and out. "God, Arlene, I'm going to come!"

I grunt and continue to fellate him. I feel the shudder start, and he says, "I can't stand this or stop it! Fuck! Fuck, what you do to me!" and he releases a torrent of warm semen down my throat. "Arlene, that was so good, but now we will have to wait."

"Yeah, but that's okay. Let me get naked, and you can return the favor." Lars looks worried, and I ask what's wrong. "I've never done that to a woman; guide me."

"Yes." I relax and lie on the bed, spread-eagle. He kisses and tweaks my nipples, then continues down. When he is close, I put my hands in his soft blond hair and pull him forward. He is tentative with his tongue and looks up at me for approval. "Put your fingers in me and continue." He is adroit at this lesson, and I begin to feel the tightening and pulses as my body reacts. I feel his erection rising beside my thigh, and I tell him to take me hard. I pull him to me and wrap my legs around his hips. We are both sweating, and he collapses on me before he climaxes.

"Sorry. The pressure on my stump was too much."

"Oh, Lars, you need to see Dr. Todd. You shouldn't have pain when it has been so many years since your amputation." I stroke his back and release my legs from his hips. "Roll onto your front," I whisper. "I'll be back in a moment." I grab some massage oil and go to the microwave in the kitchen. Thirty seconds, and the oil is warm. I return to Lars and pour a copious amount on his back, massaging as I go.

"This feels so good. Love it. And you." I kiss his shoulder and knead his muscled back, working my way down to his behind. I continue to knead and feel his body relax. His eyes are closed, and his breathing is deep. I return my hands to his back splay my fingers as I slowly circle the larger muscles. Lars is asleep. I lie down beside him and slowly rub his left forearm. Such a gentle soul. "What PTSD?" I wonder; I haven't seen any evidence of it. I kiss him, leave the bedside light on so I won't disturb him, and close my eyes. What a day.

CHAPTER ELEVEN

I feel the mattress flex and look over at the clock. 4:00 a.m. Soft, clear, blue eyes regard me, and I ask if anything is wrong. "No, but if you don't mind, I want to talk."

"Of course. Are you worried?"

"No. Sorry I fell asleep. I can just relax next to you, and I don't have to be concerned about my amputations. I never thought a beautiful woman would care about me. I had a dark soul and you have removed it. I love you. Do you think you could spend your life with me?"

"Oh, Lars, you have captured my heart, and I think we could be together forever. We have so much more to learn about each other, and I look forward to it. You are gentle and sincere; I don't see the missing parts—I only see a beautiful man with a gentle heart." I kiss him and tell him to make love to me. A gentle smile crosses his face, and he asks if I will help him to the bathroom.

"I'll just hop on my good leg and use you for balance."

I kick the rug out of the way and help him back to bed. He caresses my face and says, "Let me love you." I melt against him, and he claims me.

Full sun from the skylight, and we dress and head to the VA. "PTSD session today," I remind Lars. "We are a secret and must remain that way in front of the guys."

I ask Dr. Cross to arrange a consult with Dr. Todd and then greet Bill, Mike, and Ryan. Bill is hopeful to get back with his wife. Mike has grown above his toy vehicles and spent some time with the hospital's ambulance. Ryan has visited the burn unit here and found some additional courage after seeing others with far more invasive phosphorous burns: no nose, no teeth, no ears, and partial exposure of bone, not enough skin to cover it. His anger is just starting to recede, and Dr. Cross will attempt to get him a ride on an F-16. My group is healing; it is a warm feeling. "Okay, guys, settle down. I want to tell you a story.

"I had a hospice patient on the lower

level here; his name was John. He lost both hands in Vietnam and had cardiac disease. Patients in hospice are terminal and usually die in three to six months. John lasted nine months. I took care of him every day, feeding, dressing, bathing—anything he needed. Imagine if you didn't have hands, what you could not do. Button your shirt, pick up a fork to eat a meal, brush your teeth. Hold your dick to pee." The group chuckles, and Lars is rubbing his right hand, lucky to have it.

"Anyway, I was very fond of John and had a clandestine treat I shared with him on good days. John was wealthy and ordered on his laptop expensive underwear, sweatpants, shampoo, body wash, etc. He was always in a gown, no underwear, as you guys should know. Most nurses and CNAs don't need the complication of underwear when bathing or cleaning after an accident." Knowing looks circle the group.

"Anyway, the first time I noticed his collection of clothes, I asked him if I could dress him in his clothes. He got the biggest grin, and I walked over to him and he raised his hips so I could pull his underwear on and follow with sweatpants. It drew tears, and he said, 'It makes me feel like a man again.' Can you feel his emotion? I always had a chocolate bar for him too—broken in small pieces he could scoop up with his mouth so that no one had to feed him. Yes, John and I had a special relationship. You have to when you have to wipe his butt after a bowel movement every day. He loved stupid jokes and told me I was beautiful and that he wished he had hands to hug me. A special man. Anyway, I saw his lawyer yesterday, and John acknowledged me in his will. Twenty thousand to me be-cause he loved me." Tears begin to fall again. "Such a wonderful man, but I feel guilty to take the money, so I am donating the entire amount to Wounded Warriors."

"Fuck, yes, Arlene—what a woman!"

"Thank you, guys. I owe you all a hug." I give Bill, Mike, and Ryan a hug and kiss their foreheads. Lars patiently waits for his and caresses my backside, hidden from the others.

"See you next week. Stay strong; you are all growing on me."

Dr. Cross motions me to the hall and says he has arranged an appointment for Lars with Dr. Todd in thirty days. "That's the VA," he says. "Always too busy for a quick visit. On another note, I think we are all falling in love with you, Arlene—including me."

I hug Dr. Cross and kiss his forehead as well, winking at him. "I will see you next week."

CHAPTER TWELVE

I tell Lars I want to go downstairs to the temporary Wounded Warriors desk set up every Wednesday to garner donations from families and vets. "I'll be back to take you home." Big smile and a gentle slap to my backside.

I find the Warriors' desk and explain why I am here. The man at the desk is incredulous and says they could really use the funds and would acknowledge John's donation. I ask him to put it in the paper. "Everyone should know about John, his sacrifice and brave battle to live." I endorse the check, smile, and tell the man to, "spend it wisely. A man suffered to earn this."

I return upstairs and collect Lars. "Let's go to dinner and have a drink."

"Sounds good. I'll put on my jeans."

I balance him, zip his jeans, and admire

this blond, blue-eyed Viking, mine to love. We go to a local steakhouse and order margaritas. We talk about the future, and he wonders where we will live. I tell him, "At my house. It's paid for and I have Social Security." He offers to pitch in his VA disability, and I tell him we will have a wonderful life together, as long as we stay healthy.

"Speaking of which, Dr. Cross made an appointment for you with Dr. Todd."

His face contorts as he says, "I don't want to have more surgery." I tell him his balance will improve with a well-fitted prosthesis and that the revision surgery would most likely eliminate the pain to wear it. Lars is still anxious, and I reassure him that it is his decision. "We can talk about it again after we see Dr. Todd."

He relaxes a little, and I order another margarita for both of us. Our steaks come, and I cut my T-bone—rare and a little too bloody for me. I turn it to Lars and say, "I will send it back for a little more cooking." He has a foreign look on his face; his eyes have darkened, and he is shuddering. Alarmed, I gently ask him, "What is it, Lars?"

"The blood. The blood."

I rub his shoulder and tell him, "You

aren't in a chopper; it is animal blood. Close your eyes and relax. I am right here."

He continues to shake and squirm in his seat. Okay, PTSD has shown its fearsome face. The waiter comes over, and I ask him to have the steak cooked longer. "Well-done, no blood." I turn so I can put my arms around Lars and tell him to close his eyes and put his head on my shoulder. "You are in the U.S., having dinner with a woman who loves you."

We are getting some concerned looks from other diners, and I squeeze Lars tightly to me. He continues to shake and can't seem to talk.

"You are okay. Breathe, honey, breathe. I love you." I just hold him and wait for him to settle. The shaking subsides very slowly, and a couple of diners stop to ask if we need a doctor.

"No, we can handle it; just give us a few minutes." The waiter returns with my steak, and I signal him to wait. Lars has somewhat conquered his fear and tears roll down his smooth cheeks. He hugs me back and apologizes; he's not even sure what has happened.

I tell him, "You had an attack in response to the blood from my steak."

He closes his eyes and squeezes my

hand, telling me that he can't control these episodes.

"We will work on this. I love you, Lars, and I'm here; I will protect you."

"Arlene, I love you too. I'm sorry—can we just go home?"

Agreeing that it'd be a good idea, I signal the waiter for our check and a box for my steak. Lars is a little wobbly as I smile my thanks to the adjacent diners, so I give him his crutch and put my arm around him. "You okay?"

He stiffly nods.

"Good. We'll go home and have a hot bath." He is silent on the way home, and I caress his left thigh. I hug him in the driveway, and we slowly walk to the front door. Home sweet home.

CHAPTER THIRTEEN

I put the steak box in the fridge and tell Lars that I'm going to start the bath. He nods, still silent. I turn on the water and adjust the temperature, pour in a copious amount of bath oil, and lay a fluffy towel on the bottom of the large soaker tub. I lead Lars to the tub, and he says, "I don't know if I can get in or out of it."

"I will help you and make sure you don't fall." I am taking a risk, but I will watch him carefully. I undress him and have him sit on the edge of the tub. I peel my clothes off and tell Lars to turn around and face the tub. He obeys, and I give him my hand for support, telling him to stand and then ease down in the water. I sit behind him and put my arms around his waist, pulling him against me. I wrap my legs around his and start to circle his chest with body wash and the fragrant hot water, and he leans his head on my chest.

"Relax, relax, Lars. I'm here and will keep you safe."

"Kiss me, Arlene. Kiss me hard." I do and feel his rapid heartbeat against me.

"What are you thinking?"

"I'm ashamed. I'm sorry, Arlene."

"Lars, you have nothing to be ashamed about, nothing. You had some horrible things happen to you in Nam. Your brain short-circuits sometimes and sends you back. You haven't overcome the fear, but you will. Nam was so many years ago, but memories can transport you back, I am your lifejacket and will tighten the straps and make you safe. I love you." He tries to turn and give me a hug and slips a little.

"Okay, time for bed." I help him up and sit him on the tub edge again and tell him to wait for me to get out; "don't try it on your own." I turn him to face me and swing his leg and the foreshortened stump. I put my arm around him and ease him up to standing. He starts to shiver, so I wrap a fluffy towel around his shoulders and lead him to the bed. I pull the covers over us until he is warm again. I tell him to sleep. He shakes his head and says,

"No, I need to make love to you. "Okay, but fuck me hard. Let some of that poison out of you." He gently gets on top of me and says, "Grab my ass and pull me deep into you." I pull him into me and apply strong pressure to his backside, driving his cock into me at a furious pace. He is panting, breathing heavy, and continues to pound into me. I wrap my legs around him and place my ankles under the cheeks of his ass to keep pressure on him.

"Oh, God, Arlene, oh, God. I need you." "And I need you too, Lars. Let me have it; you need to come. Fill me; come for me." He climaxes, the sweat dripping on my chest. "Fuck. Fuck, that was so good. It's your Viking blood, my blond warrior." I kiss him and tell him to sleep, sleep. I kiss his eyes and tell him sweet dreams. Gradually, his breathing returns to normal, and he is asleep.

CHAPTER FOURTEEN

I kiss his eyes and tell him sweet dreams. Gradually, his breathing returns to normal, and he is asleep. On the other hand, I am restless, reviewing the events. It was scary and happened so quickly. No warning for Lars and a surprise for me. I will question Dr. Cross. I watch his chest rise and fall and smooth his soft blond hair off his forehead. What I feel for this damaged man, it frightens me, the cost of freedom. Freedom, hell. Vets are prisoners to their past, many missing parts of it. I tell my brain to shut down; it is time to sleep. I wiggle up against Lars, safe and sound. A grin on my face when I feel his member against my ass.

"Hey. Good morning, sleepyhead." Two clear blue eyes open and scan my face; a smile develops, and he says, "I'm sorry." "It is after ten. Scoot your butt over here, and I'll dress

hot water, squirt some soap on the wash-cloth, and keel behind him, gently separating his cheeks and clean the residue from his behind. "God, I hate being an invalid." "You aren't; you just need a little help." I rinse the washcloth out and finish the job. Pinching his butt, I say, "All clean; now I just need to get you up."

"You will need to help me with that."

"Put your hand on the tub edge and try to get your good leg under you and stand." We make several attempts, but Lars is not able to lift his body enough to stand. He is sweating and panting.

"Hold still. I have an idea." I go to the kitchen and return with a low single-step stool. Lars looks confused, so I tell him, "If I can get you a little higher onto the stool, it will be easier to get you upright. Try hard, because if this doesn't work, I'll have to call an ambulance for help."

"Fuck, fuck, I'm useless!"

I ignore him and tell him to push hard against my foot so I can pressure his good leg enough to balance him and raise him up the seven inches we need to the stool. I sit in front of him and place his bare foot against mine. "Push off with your good arm when I put pressure on your leg." It doesn't work the first few times we try, and I smile, thinking about the contortionist games kids play.

"Again, push hard, Lars." He is straining but off the floor a few inches. I quickly grab his hips and get him to the stool. We are both sweating and gulping for air. I kiss him and tell him to rest for a few minutes. I grab a clean washcloth and cold water and swab his face and mine.

"We can do this, Lars—fuck an ambulance! Now what I want to do is use your good leg and arm and try to stand but then sit on the edge of the tub before you are standing." He nods his understanding, and we get him to the tub edge. "Rest, rest, I'll get you up in a moment." His face is blotched with red from the strain, but he smiles and nods his head.

"Okay, let's get you up. Put your hand on my shoulder; my arms will bear-hug you and help you up. Push with your good leg and stand." With the second surge, we are successful, and he is upright on his foot. I lean over and nest his crutch under his armpit. "Stay still till you feel balanced and tell me if you are feeling lightheaded." Again, he nods, dips his head, and kisses my shoulder.

We hold each other for several minutes,

trembling from exertion. He whispers, "I'm okay now," and we creep back to the bed. He falls forward onto the mattress, and I swing his leg and stump onto it. I crawl in and pull the covers over both of us, my front against his back.

CHAPTER FIFTEEN

Lars's pulse slows, and I caress his belly, gradually lowering my hand to his genitals.

"I don't think I can do this now."

"No, I just want to hold you close," and I squeeze him tighter. He drifts off to sleep, and I relive the struggle we went through to get him up. We both need to get a little stronger, and I need to talk to an occupational therapist for tips to get Lars upright again if he falls. A gait belt wouldn't help; it's just an unusual combination of one leg and one hand on opposite sides needing to coordinate movement together. I kiss his shoulder and roll out of bed. I need coffee, and he needs some rest.

Will I always be a caregiver? It's what I know—ups and downs—but I love this man and the pull to help strangles the doubt. Yes,

I will always be a caregiver because that is what I do: I care. I care. I hear Lars call me, and I gulp the last of my coffee and head to the bedroom, yelling for him not to get up until I'm there.

I lie down beside Lars and tell him we need to talk. He sighs and says, "I'm so sorry."

"No need to be; just give me a moment to brush my teeth, and I'll be right back beside you." I brush my teeth and return to a concerned Lars. "What are you worried about?"

"I couldn't help falling, and I hated that you had to clean my ass."

"Oh, Lars, you have a great ass! Now I just know it a little better." Just to emphasize the point, I smack him gently and then kiss his backside. Reaching up, I clasp his head and kiss him deeply.

"I'm not ready to talk about yesterday; I'm still unsettled from this morning."

"Just relax. I'll call the hospital and tell them to cancel your rehab for the day, and you can spend it with me."

"Can we fuck? I need a diversion."

"Sure, feel okay, Lars?"

He nods and reaches for my breasts. He trails kisses down my throat and sternum and tells me to grab his cock. An invitation I will

Katherine Zartman

never refuse, I feel his firmness and guide him home. He is slow and gentle with me until I urge him to let loose. He sets a fast, furious pace and moans my name. Now frantic, he loses control, and I grip him hard as his semen is squirting all over me.

"I don't know what is wrong with me today; help me understand!"

"I don't have an answer, Lars; I just think you are anxious and embarrassed over how the unknown has conflicted you. We handled your attack at dinner, as well as your fall this morning. We just need to trust each other and know that we need and love each other. Besides, you really do have a great ass, Lars." I wink at him, see a smile, and head into the bathroom to get a warm washcloth as we are both a bit sticky. Noticing the laundry pile on the floor, I load the strays into the basket, set it by the bed, and kiss Lars again. He swats my behind and gives me a carnal look, his blue eyes heated, his blond hair tousled in disarray.

"Don't go anywhere—I'm just going to put the laundry in the washer."

He smirks and says, "I didn't quite get it in the right place last time."

"Yeah, well, gunners have been known

66

to miss sometimes. They get too excited and miss the target."

He laughs, and I head to the washer. Why not spend the day in bed? We deserve it and could have a wonderful afternoon. I return to the bedroom, and Lars is in the bathroom, crutch under his arm and holding on to a grip bar by the tub.

"I'm a little unsteady myself at times," I say as I walk over and hold his cock steady, so he doesn't spray all over. "Ready for another?" He smiles and says, "Am I ever. I just had to pee first." I slip my arm around his waist, kick the bathroom rug away so his crutch doesn't catch, and return to bed. He kisses me deeply, exploring my mouth and running his tongue along my teeth. He whispers to me, "I want to make you come. I have done a poor job pleasing you, so let me." "Oh, Lars, you please me all the time, but I'm more than ready for you to please me that way."

CHAPTER SIXTEEN

He snakes his hand down over my breasts and belly, ruffles my pubic hair, and asks for some oil as he tickles my clitoris. He establishes a rhythm back and forth, back and forth, then pushes his palm against me. I am soon panting, and I can feel his erection rising against my thigh. "Put your cock in me, and we can come together." He rolls on top of me and tells me to put it in, he doesn't want to let go of me. "God, you feel so good, I could stay here all day,"" No, I can't last that long." "Neither can I," and he tips over the edge. Both of us panting, sweating and he shouts "Fuck, Arlene! I can't hold it anymore." "Let go. Let me feel you shudder through it." He collapses on me, kissing my neck, and says, "I'm hungry. I didn't have breakfast." "How about a cheese omelet and sourdough toast?" "Perfect, and maybe a massage for dessert." "Dessert? Who has dessert for breakfast?" God, this man I love. "Stay here—I'll bring you breakfast in bed." I walk to the kitchen, pull out a pan for the omelet, and grate some cheese and mix it with eggs. I ponder warming the steak from dinner and decide against it. I chop some green onions and add it to the bubbling eggs. They need a few minutes, so I throw clothes in the dryer and pop the toast in, butter, honey, locate a serving tray, and check to see if the coffee is still hot. Cloth napkin, a good white plate, a rose snapped from the vase in the living room, and I slide the hot omelet to a plate. Coffee with creamer, and his tray is ready to go. I enter the bedroom, fluff some pillows behind Lars, and place the tray over his thighs. "Smells great, and I love honey on my toast." He digs in, and I steal a piece of toast from the plate, "Hey, that's mine." "No, ours. Something you need to get used to." "You are like a mom to me." "No, Lars, just because I wiped your ass this morning does not make me your mom." His face falls, so I kiss him and remind him that he has a great ass. A smile emerges, and I ask him what he has in mind for dessert. "You naked in the bed. "Let me go get the clothes out of the dryer, and I'll be back to serve dessert." I gather the warm clothes and return to the bedroom and fold, sort, and put away the clothes. I put a CD in the player, and the soft sounds of Billie Holliday wrap around me and the room. "Hurry up, baby. I need you" I have a sudden thought: I need to make some room for Lars, clothes, shoes. It won't take long as he needs only a left one. I wonder what he does with the right one in a pair. Could be a good business, selling single shoes to vets. *What size and left or right?* I clamp down on those morbid thoughts and bring a warm, soapy washcloth to the bed. I clean Lars up and run it over my sex as well. I rinse the cloth and return to remove soap from Lars. "I don't want to taste soap, just you." He smiles and tips his hips up. Something else is rising as well. So, I close my mouth around his member and begin to draw him in and out. I circle the tip, and he groans, pressing it farther in; soon he is panting and motions for me to sit on him. I place him in me and wait for his tender stroking to begin. He surprises me when he grips my ass and pushes it up and down as his hips flex and relax, a genetic trait the body knows well. We continue, and I feel the now-familiar shuddering begin; he shifts slightly and places his right hand on my hip and tries to get his left arm stump on my other hip. It slides off, and he attempts it again. "Lars just use your right, and I'll do the rest." Yeah, those Kegel exercises do work. The shuddering is becoming more frantic, and he voices, loudly, "I'm going to come." I shift my weight forward and kiss his chest; he is exploding in me, and I feel the moisture tracking down my inner thighs. I muzzle his ear and whisper, "My love." He whispers in return, "I love you too, so much it scares me."

"What scares you?

"Change. Blood. The fear of my PTSD. I never know what triggers it and how to stop an attack. I knew last night I was having an attack, but I was powerless to stop it. My brain floods with images, and I smell the pungent odor of blood. I can't talk, I can't move, all I can do is surrender to the power it has on my body."

"Keep talking, Lars; tell me your darkest thoughts while you are lying next to me."

"I remember we were coming into an LZ under fire. We hit the ground, incoming rounds ping against the UH-1, so I ratchet the M-60, full of ammo, and grip it tightly as I see a platoon gathering wounded to come aboard. NVA troops are advancing on the LZ; I fire, and watch bodies fall. Two more burst through the thick undergrowth, and I shoot them quickly and motion for our guys to bring the wounded. The most critical first, no stretchers, only soldiers as this LZ is newly made," He stops to catch his breath and continues his story in staccato tones. "The three soldiers advancing to the chopper are cut down from the back by a mortar round. I sweep the area where I saw a flash of light, and two more soldiers limp toward the UH-1. Again, a mortar stops them, and another burst in front of me. I feel a sharp pain in my neck, and then everything goes black. I learned later I had no right leg, my neck was damaged from shrapnel, and my left hand was to be amputated the next morning. The LZ had become too hot, the chopper was damaged, the five soldiers coming to the craft were killed, and aircraft was able to limp back to the base, carrying the only wounded we saved, me and the copilot. The pilot died from a stray round as we were leaving. Six dead. I would be better to be the same. I had failed." "You didn't fail, Lars. You were never caught in a battle enemy forces had in their favor and with more weapons. You were very lucky to have survived." "Yeah, does it look like I survived?" He holds up his stumps. "Yeah, lucky." "There are thousands who lost more than you have. I know, I have cared for many of them." I think of John, and tears fall again. "Oh, Lars, you are alive. A complete man to me. I love you. Don't let words become bullets." He kisses me and says, "I need a drink." Knowing I need to lighten the mood I ask, "How about pizza and a beer. I have beer, and I'll order the pizza; what kind would you like? Anchovies?" "Ugh, I hate anchovies. Norsemen and their taste for anything fish." "So, pepperoni and cheese it is." Lars laughs again, and I tell him "I'll throw in a movie, your choice." "*Lord of the Rings*. Yes, I have it, a little Frodo, no pun intended." I call and order the pizza and bring a bottle of beer to Lars. The pizza comes when Lars is on his second beer, and I put the pizza and roll of paper towels on the bed. I prop up the pillows again for Lars and sit cross-legged. Lars, of course, cannot. I turn on the Blu-ray and play the movie; soon Frodo and Bilbo are off on their adventure. Hobbits are so far removed from the battle of Vietnam; I hope a good distraction for Lars. We each have several pieces of pizza, and I join him with my first beer; he is on his third. I wipe his face because he is sporting a tomato sauce chin, and he says, "This is fun. I can't see a movie at the VA unless I go to the communal lounge; it's too noisy, and the guys are loud—hard to follow and hear dialog." "Lars, as soon as you are on outpatient status, we can do this all the time and have sex whenever we want." "Baby, I can't wait. Are you sure you want to be saddled with my burden?" "You aren't a burden; you are a joy." "Like this morning I was." "It will get easier all the time for both of us."

CHAPTER SEVENTEEN

"By the way, Lars, do you have a storage unit or things somewhere I need to make room for?" "No, just what is in my closet at the VA. Clothes, letters, and a few CDs."

"Do you have any photos?"

"Yes, pictures of my family, my brother who died, as you know, and pictures of Norway."

"Great, I can't wait to see them. Lars, this will be your home too; anything you want to change or need, just tell me."

"Yeah, get rid of that fucking rug in the bathroom." I laugh, and I start the movie where I paused it.

"I need to pee."

"Three beers, I'm sure you do,"

"Throw out the fucking rug and hold my cock for me. I like it when you do."

"Yes, I like it too."

"That's my girl."

"My stamina is back, and I want you again."

"I want to take you from behind—it will be easier for me to balance, and I will be able to feel your ass against me." We return to the room, and I pause the movie again. I really should just turn it off. I lie down on my stomach, and he mounts me; his full weight presses me to the mattress. He trails kisses down my spine and uses his right hand to guide his cock into me. The initial thrust is gentle; the following ones increase with intensity. "I need this, baby."

"Tell me if I hurt you."

"I will; push it as hard as you like." He does. The frantic coupling continues, and he yells through his release, "Fuck, Arlene, I love this and you."

"You're becoming insatiable, Lars. I love it too." He kisses my shoulder, and his face is wet. I roll over and hug him strongly. We don't talk, both understanding the passion that requires no conversation. Tears continue, further our voices with a deep kiss. Sleep, sleep, sweet Lars, pleasant dreams. I pull the covers and snuggle against him. The warm length of his body is like a sedative to me.

CHAPTER EIGHTEEN

I t is Wednesday, a PTSD meeting at 1:00, and I need to return Lars to the hospital. I talk to Dr. Cross before the others arrive and ask when Lars can be released to outpatient status.

"How do you think he is, Arlene?"

"Well, he had an attack a few days ago, and we are working it out; a silly trigger brought it on."

He questions what triggered the attack.

"A bloody rare steak at dinner."

"Yes, it makes sense. Blood is one of his warnings, born from revulsion of his blood in the helicopter when he was wounded. PTSD is a convoluted illness, different for every patient, and we have no cure, no magic pill, just gentle understanding until the memories are overtaken by something else."

CHAPTER NINETEEN

"**C**ome, let's go visit the guys." I sit next to Bill, and he hugs me. "Arlene, I'm going to remarry my wife. We talked, and she has listened. No anger on my part anymore. We even had sex again. It was mind-blasting for me, and you were the reason it happened. Thank you for your words and touch. I never imagined a woman like you could be so important—you see into me, not missing arms, legs, burns. Fuck, Ryan is a nightmare. How can you stand it?"

"Bill, I only see your tortured souls and reach out to them with a touch." Mike is quiet and clutches a model ambulance and shuttle van. He starts to tell me he now has a job driving vets to and from the hospital; he is animated, but speech is clearly hard for this man. I kiss his forehead and tell him to drive safe. Ryan taps his forehead. "Me too." I kiss him and feel the tortured skin, rough against my lips. He doesn't want to talk today, just sit by me and hold my hand. His eyes scan Lars; he holds up my hand in triumph, and Lars gives him the finger. "Okay, you two, be nice." Dr. Cross comes over and hands Lars a sheet of paper; he reads, smiles, and hands it to me. "Released to outpatient status. Effective today." He pulls my hand to his lips and says, "Fuck you, guys. I'm out of here," and pulls me toward the door. I call out good-bye to the group, now down to three. I open his locker and begin to pull out Lars's meager belongings. How sad to see twenty years of life gathered in a heap on a discharge cart; it is punctuated with two prosthesis on top. I pull his wheelchair over, and he sits down, dropping his crutch. All patients discharged leave in a wheelchair or a body bag. Lars says, "I'm so fucking happy to get out of here; it has been a grind." I kiss his head in front of me and reach back to pull the cart with us. I need to push the wheelchair because Lars, with only one hand, cannot control the steering. No fancy wheelchair here, just a service-able basic to save the taxpayers money. He stops me by putting his foot down when we approach the large exit doors. "What is it, Lars?"

"I just want to be sure you are okay with this; I don't want to be a hardship on you."

"There is only one thing I want hard from you, Lars." He laughs and says, "Then get me home." I pull into a liquor store on the way home and buy some champagne. We will celebrate his escape from the hospital and all the horrors that it possesses. I go over some of the details I will need to change to make living with Lars easier for both of us. More grip bars, enlarging the shower, a walk-in tub would be great, another chest of drawers for his clothes, add him to my gym membership, change some of the thresholds in the house and whatever Lars would like. I am not daunted by the challenges ahead; I am excited to have this fragile Viking with me twenty-four hours a day. "You're home, Lars." He smiles and says, "Can't wait to celebrate."

CHAPTER TWENTY

I leave him sitting on *our* bed and go to retrieve his belongings. "I want to pee." I smile, and he grips the support bar. I grip his cock. "Yeah, I could get used to this." I should make sure the support bar is good and strong—no falls again. I get him back to the bed, now ours, and pick up the bathroom rug. "Here to be banished from this bath." He smiles and says, "Come here. I need to make love to you." Our kiss is hungry as I tug his T-shirt off and pull down his sweatpants. Already hard in anticipation, he squeezes a breast, and I pull him to my mouth. "No, baby, I want to be in you." I release him and guide him to the entrance door of his new home. "Welcome home, Lars." He moves through the door and adjusts to the space. Pressing, pulling, twisting, he is passionate. I pull him in farther when I force his ass forward. Panting, his breath labored, and he releases his happiness at being home.

"Fuck, baby, what a great welcome mat! I love you."

"I love you too, Lars, and I am ready to share everything life brings to us. Joy, tears, loss, and memories—you complete me."

"Oh, baby, my tears are to show you how much more of a man I am now. You have replaced my missing parts, and I am whole again."

God, could I love this man more!? We lie together for what seems like hours, gently caressing each other and content with our destiny laid out before us. "Come, I want to explore the house with you, so you can tell me what changes will help you when you're in your wheelchair so that I can see if you can get through doorways or around furniture placement."

"Why do we need to do that?"

"Lars, there will be times when you are in the house alone, and I want you to be comfortable and able to manage."

"When will I be alone?"

"If I'm grocery shopping, running errands, etc. And I will be gone a few hours a week at the hospital. I quit work, but I will volunteer my time to help a few more broken men, no shortages there."

"God, Arlene, you've been a caregiver for so long—haven't you seen enough?"

"No, Lars, it's the way I am—I can't refuse when I see something broken."

He is quiet for a few seconds and then softly asks, "Am I still broken?"

"No, Lars, you are just bent a little. A few cracks that need some more glue."

He smiles. "Such a good woman."

I kiss him. "Such a good man."

What is it about couples deeply in love and at a mature age—they become excited teenagers all over again. Well, since we are both above the legal drinking age, I open the champagne and pour us a glass.

"Push me into the living room and sit on the couch beside me." He grabs my hand and brings it to his lips, softly kissing it multiple times. His blue eyes are bright and full of promise. I turn to him, and he pats his lap, gesturing for me to sit down.

"Tell me if I'm too heavy." He nods, and I gently sit down on him, placing my arms around him. After a few minutes, he softly whispers, "We are not married but bound together, and I will do my part to hold us together. I want to go to the bank and open a joint account and have the lawyer create a new will, as you are my life now."

I hug him tighter, shift a little to ease my weight on his legs, and tell him to make love to me. We get comfortable on the bed, and Lars covers my body with soft kisses. Rubbing back and forth across my belly, he notices some small scars. "What are those from?"

"I had surgery to remove my gallbladder and also had a tubal."

"What is that?"

CHAPTER TWENTY-ONE

explain that I'm sterile, no more kids. His face falls, and he says, "I always wanted some."

"Oh, Lars, I'm way too old to have any more kids, even if I could. We will visit my kids, grandkids, and great-granddaughter. When we are done here, I can show you some photo albums." He smiles and says, "Well, let's get to it."

He covers me, and now familiar enough with my body, he needs no guiding hand. I grip his ass and pull him home. He rises and falls, rises and falls, increasing the tempo with every stroke. I feel the flexing of his good arm and his shoulders. They vibrate and then begin to shudder, as does his cock. He climaxes loudly. "Fuck. Fuck. Fuck." A tremor runs through me, and he rolls to his side. He tickles my clitoris and presses the back of his hand against it, alternating with his fingers. I begin to shake harder and convulse as my climax rolls through my pelvis and belly. "I don't do that enough for you. I promise I will do it more often. Did you think I made love to you?"

"Oh, Lars, you are so dear to me and show your love and new confidence every day. Your body and brain are waking from a long period of just existing in a hospital bed. Now you are in *our* bed, a new man, one I love and admire."

"Yes, baby, you're right. I am a dark fairy tale come to life; the hundreds of dreams I had are unbelievable, coming true, replacing the nightmares." I kiss him and squeeze his cock. He says, "No, too sore."

"I know I just wanted to hold it." He pulls me up and says, "Come, show me your kids and tell me what I should know before I meet them."

"You will like my son-in-law; he is Norwegian too. Not tall, not blond. A gentle soul, technically advanced, and a caring father. My daughter will be forceful and fun trying to dig into your brain. She is in the mental field, and you will become a project for her. Freyja is extremely sweet and smart, loves rocks and the outside. She has a Norwegian name. Yes, when we get our husky, we will name him Zeus." He laughs and says, "I always wanted one, but he can't share our bed."

"No, we need to change it to a king; a queen is fine for one, but a king is better for a big guy like you and occasionally a big gray-and-white husky." Again, Lars, laughs and says, "So quickly my future has changed, and you have done this."

"We have done this."

CHAPTER TWENTY-TWO

He picks up a photo from the bookcase and asks, "Who is this?" A young boy with white-blond hair and blue eyes stare back at the grown man who looks like him as an adult. I laugh and say, "The blond hair is gone; he is bald now. That is Tony, my youngest son. He is a grandpa, and I am a great-grandma. You will like him, and I know he will like you. You can go fishing with him or maybe elk hunting once we get your revision down on your leg." He frowns and says, "No more surgery. I have lost enough."

"Lars, they may not have to take any more of the leg, just get the flap more comfortable, so you can use a prosthesis without pain. Don't worry—we can take our time, and you will have the final decision; it is your leg."

"In Vietnam, after the original surgery, I had a roommate, Joe, who lost a leg out in the field. He had an amputation below the knee, but one morning they came for him. After the surgery, his leg was cut much shorter, only to the middle of his thigh."

"Lars, in Vietnam, it was a very recent amputation, sometimes in the field to save a life; perhaps he had an infection or poor circulation and the surgeons needed to remove more to save him. You are not at all in that situation, and Dr. Todd will explain in detail what he can and cannot do, if you decide." I kiss him and kiss his stump.

"I'm afraid, baby."

"I know. Don't be afraid—it is only a possibility, and if it happens, you know I will be right beside you, loving you as I do now." He pulls me close, and I squeeze him back. He starts to shake, and tears roll down his face. "I'm afraid, I'm afraid." I pull him in and sit in a chair, calming him on my lap like a small child. I rock him back and forth, and he leans his head on my shoulder, the tears still flowing. "Oh, this poor, poor damaged man." I feel my own tears begin and rock him harder. The ravages of war cannot stay dormant without hidden scars. He raises his head and says, "I want to lie down beside you. No sex, just love." We lie down and spoon together. My back to his front, and he snakes his right arm around my waist and pulls the left stump to his right hand to squeeze me tighter. He kisses my back and starts to cry again. I tell him, "Let loose; cry as much as you need—I'm here." He is racked by huge sobs. "Baby, I don't, I can't, I don't."

"I know, I know, just cry it out. I'm here for you." His nose is running, and he wipes it on his pillow and slowly kisses my shoulder. We stay tightly together until the heat from our bodies forces us apart. He is calm now, so I tell him that we will be going to my son's house for dinner tomorrow night. "It is time you two meet; he also has three dogs that go crazy when they see me." We spend a quiet day, and then Lars seems nervous in the afternoon. "What if he doesn't like me?"

"He will love you because he loves his mama, and he just wants her to be happy, and you qualify for that."

"Do I need the wheelchair, or can I just use my crutch?"

"Crutch. He has stairs, which I will help you negotiate."

We park in front of my son's house; I kiss Lars. The dogs are at the window, barking already. I tell Lars, "Let me get Tony to put Ghost away so he doesn't knock you down."

"Who is Ghost?"

"A large, all-white German shepherd who tends to get overly friendly. He has almost knocked me down several times." I go up to the door and greet the dogs—Ghost, as predicted, is all over me. Domino, a miniature pinscher, is squawking like a parrot, and Adonis, another miniature pinscher, is excited too, as most puppies are. Tony offers to help me with Lars and the few stairs leading up to the house. Ghost first refuses to go to his kennel, but after a few more commands, he obediently goes to his kennel in the living room and lies down. Now, he won't come out until Tony gives a release command. We head out to the car and collect Lars. I introduce Tony. "This is the little, white, blond, blue-eyed kid I showed you a picture of."

"Oh yes, and I see now, bald." Lars extends his hand to shake; Tony shakes it and says, "Finally, I meet Mom's boyfriend."

I pull the crutch from the back of the car, and we go to the house. Tony steadies Lars, and we are greeted by a few growls from Ghost. Tony silences him, and I tell Lars to go ahead and sit down before Tony releases him.

On command and still growling a bit, Ghost leaps up on the couch to lick my face and investigate the stranger beside me. He creeps over my lap to sniff Lars, and Lars pets his head and rubs his ears. "This dog is huge! And beautiful."

"You just made a friend." The other two dogs are soon in my lap, trained by the alpha not to interfere when he is getting attention. Tony comes over and talks about his latest fishing trip and gets some background on Lars. Then he starts the barbeque and the steaks, sweet potatoes, and homemade sourdough bread; he makes several loaves every week. The large seventy-inch TV is on, and we watch Sunday night football, one of my favorite pastimes, and the Bears and the Cowboys are playing. Lars likes football too, though no real preference on teams.

I talk about when I was stationed at Corpus Christi, working in avionics and with frequent duty in the paraloft. We were a training squadron, receiving pilots from jet training in Jacksonville, Florida. The pilots needed training in props before being deployed in Vietnam. I mention that we were also a major facility for helicopters damaged in Nam. Should I have Lars hear this? Would it upset him? Tony volunteers a few comments, so I know Lars really hears the story. I smile, kiss him, and go on, telling him we would get shipments in periodically to repair, rob parts, and get those helicopters back in service.

"Unfortunately, Lars, many of them were Bell Huey's, UH-1's, desperately needed in Vietnam. Five thousand of them and a few thousand of the earlier versions—work-horses for landing in the LZs to pick up the wounded." Lars is very silent, so I stop talking and kiss him. Ghost barks and comes over to lick my face again; spoiled dog but so love-able. We turn back to the game. Dallas scores again and has the lead going into halftime. Soon, dinner is ready, and we negotiate the full plates as Tony brings over a folding table to make access for Lars easier.

"Great steak, Tony, and I love your bread."

Third quarter, and Dallas is intercepted. The dogs are restless, and Ghost pulls a dirty football out of his kennel. He loves to play catch all the time, so Tony stands and invites us to go outside. We stand, and the dogs are out of the doggie door and into the yard like a flash. We go out the slider, and Lars asks what the little building on the deck is.

"A sauna and my hot tub. You should try

it: heated water, massage, jets, and I have extra trunks." Lars looks at me and sighs, and I explain to Tony the message Lars was conveying to me. "Tony, Lars wouldn't be able to get in and out with his balance issues."

"Okay, I'm sorry. I didn't think."

Ghost breaks in with a dirty football in his mouth and brings it to Lars to throw. Lars tosses it over the high wall behind the hot tub and rocks a little sideways, his crutch falling to the deck. Tony is beside him and luckily prevents a fall. Ghosts returns, and I toss the ball for him, though he drops it at Lars's foot. We return to the living room, where we see that the Bears have now scored, and we talk about going up to Blue Lake to go trout fishing. But again, it would be problematic for Lars to be able to get in and out of the boat.

"I really think this is why you need revision surgery and a better prosthesis. Then you have two legs to balance you and make you able to do things you can't do with just the one leg and no left hand."

CHAPTER TWENTY-THREE

ars groans a little and rubs his stomach. Time to go. Tony grips Lars's shoulder and says, "Look forward to our next visit, and I love to see Mama so happy." I tell the doggies I'll see them soon, and we head home. Lars continues to hold his stomach, so I ask him what's wrong.

"I'm constipated and don't feel well."

"Hmm. Too many pain pills, maybe. When did you last have a bowel movement?" He estimates around four or five days ago, so we stop so I can get some MiraLAX and Gatorade for him, stating that he needs to drink more fluids. We get home, and I put him to bed, kiss him, and tell him to wake me if he has to go. No such luck and when he tries in the morning, no results. I feel his stomach; definitely some distention there. I go to the store and pick up more Gatorade along with some strong suppositories, adding a fleet enema to the purchase. If he is impacted, these probably won't work, but I'll try, knowing that Lars will be shy and embarrassed.

When I get home, I place the shopping bag on the bed, and Lars tells me that he's miserable, and the pain is getting worse. I tell him we will try the suppositories first since they more likely to work. He groans and asks, "What do I need to do?"

"Just relax. I'll take care of it. Roll on your side." I pull his sweatpants down, and he says, "No, I can't do this."

"Relax, Lars; it will only take a moment." I hold him steady, separate his cheeks, and insert a suppository.

"Fuck, I hate this."

"You are going to hate it even more if this doesn't work; we'll see." By the morning, the suppository hasn't worked, and he is doubled over in pain. I sit down on the bed and tell him that he is impacted and that I need to do an extraction.

"What the fuck is that?"

I explain the procedure and that I've done it several times in my hospice work. He grimaces and tells me no, to which I respond that either I can do it here or he'll have to go to the VA and have a stranger do it. I finally convince him that it is the only way to relieve the pain.

"Okay, let's get it over with."

I go and collect the supplies I need: gloves, garbage bag and trash can, lubricant, hot, soapy water, and a supply of old towels. Lars is very anxious, so I add two of his anti-anxiety meds to his Gatorade. I give him his pills and explain the procedure to him again while I wait for the meds to take effect. I strip the bed down to the bottom sheet and put absorbent pads down on the bed with a few extras nearby on the table. Lars is watching me carefully and keeps repeating how much he hates this. I tell him it's not something needed very often but, again, probably the best way to help him.

I roll him onto his side with the good leg and hike up his stump to ease the angle better. I kiss him and say, "Now, this IS going to hurt, so yell if you need to, and I'll try to be as gentle as I can." I pull a pair of gloves on, squirt a copious amount of lubricant on them and spread his cheeks, telling him to try not to move out of position. I insert two fingers into his anus as he groans with discomfort. I spread my fingers and swirl them around a bit to enlarge and relax his already puckering anus. I can't feel the mass, so I know I have to go further up his colon to start to retrieve the shit. I warn him again about the pain, much greater this time as I will have to insert my entire hand to get high enough into his colon. "Take a deep breath, Lars."

I put additional lubricant all over the glove and gently force my hand much higher into his colon.

"Fuck, that hurts!"

"I know; hang on." I feel the impaction and begin to draw it forward toward his anus. Lars starts to wiggle a bit as he asks how much longer. "Ten or fifteen minutes for me to get it all out." I grab one of the absorbent pads and draw the first bit out onto it.

"Fuck, that smell."

"Yes." I smile. "Shit usually does."

I drop the pad into the garbage bag, along with the gloves as I don't want to return any of the waste to him. Donning fresh gloves and lubricant again, I insert my hand, scraping and pulling the rock-hard mass from his quivering body. He yells out again as I fill another pad. "Lars, I need to go up a little more to get the top of the mass. Take a deep breath; almost done." I flex my hand and fingers until I feel the top of the mass and pull harshly to get it out of him. He yelps and exclaims, "Thank God; are you done now?" I pull the last of the shit out and onto a pad and drop it into the garbage along with the gloves. He is quivering, and I grab a washcloth and the warm, soapy water, and I clean any residue from his behind. I bend and kiss it as he starts to turn and say, "Wait, I'm not quite done." I put the gloves on again and spread lubricant gently on his anus. It will be sore for a day or two, but he will feel so much better. Done again, I wipe my hand on one of the towels and smack his ass playfully. "Sorry I had to do that to you, but better me than someone else, right?" He gives me a ghost of a smile, and I pull the pad out from under him and throw it in the trash. "Give me a minute to throw this in the can outside, and then I'll be back to you. Don't try to get up on your own." He murmurs, and I go outside to throw away the now-full garbage bag.

I return to the bedroom and grab a pair of sweatpants for Lars. "Raise your hips, and I'll get you dressed." Tears have streaked his cheeks, so I grab his face in my hands and tell him. "I'm so sorry I had to do that. I know it was embarrassing and painful for you. I love you, Lars." I kiss him, put his sweatpants on him, and lie down beside him, my front to his back.

"Fuck. I hope I never, ever have to go through that again, but I'm glad it was you and not a stranger." I hug him hard and run my hand over his belly to see if there is any distention still there. Nice and flat.

He pulls my hand down to his cock, and I say, "No way, Lars. You have just had a traumatic experience, and you need to rest."

"No, I don't want sex; I just want you to hold it because it comforts me."

I squeeze him and tell him to close his eyes and rest. I pull the covers up with my other hand and kiss his shoulders. Oh, the love I have for this sensitive man. The trust he placed in me to allow such an invasive procedure. God, I love him.

CHAPTER TWENTY-FOUR

The next morning, we have coffee, and he wants a shower. I tell him to go sit on the toilet while I change the bed. He looks at me funny, and I tell him he might have a little more to empty. He grimaces, and I tell him not to strain too much as his ass is sore. He comes out and says, "Yeah, you were right. Now I really want a shower."

I turn the shower on and put a nonslip mat in front of the shower seat, hang two towels on nearby hooks, and grab a few washcloths. I stand in the back of the shower seat and start to soap his back and under-arms. I ask him to stand briefly, so I can clean his backside, and he says, "What is it about my ass?"

"It is about all of you, but I know your ass inside and out." He laughs, and I come around to his front and wash his cock and legs. He asks if he can wash me, and I respond, "Whatever you can do while sitting."

Soon we are both clean and shiver until dry. Relaxing on the bed, Lars says, "These sheets are so soft."

"Cuddle Duds flannel—it is starting to get colder at night."

"Well, let me warm you up and make love to you."

I kiss him deeply, and he runs his hand down my belly and twirls his fingers in my sex as he says, "Remember, I don't do this often enough."

"I remember. Continue."

He says, "Maybe I should pay you back and use my fist."

"Nooo, I don't think so. Just continue what you are doing." I give myself over to his hand and climax before I want to. He is getting too good at this; now to return the favor. I sit up and trail kisses down his body, take him in my mouth, and suck hard. My teeth graze the little ridges and indentations, and he begins to moan. I move to lie on my back, and he pulls me around.

"No, I want you on top." I settle onto him, and we work together to bring him pleasure.

"Fuck, baby, I need this—and you."

"We need each other, Lars. I love you," and he climaxes.

We dress, and I make grilled cheese sandwiches and tomato soup—soothing American comfort food for two.

CHAPTER TWENTY-FIVE

I call my daughter and tell her I want to come for a visit with Lars. "About time, Mom; we are anxious to meet your Norwegian."

"And he is anxious to meet you and the girls."

Days later, Lars and I fly out to California and rent a car. We will stay in a nearby hotel because their house has stairs, and we need a ground floor unit with grab bars. At my daughter's home that evening, her husband, Sean, hugs Lars in greeting. The girls, a bit intimidated by Lars's handicaps, shyly kiss his cheek. Turning to the youngest, Lars says, "And this must be Freyja."

His speech has taken on a slight Norwegian accent. Yoshi, their little fox dog, is happy to see me and jumps in my lap. "Sorry, buddy, no liver treats today." I excuse myself and join Sean in the kitchen to help with dinner, leaving my daughter out to get to know Lars. Eliza, my older granddaughter, arrives from school and escapes into the living room to avoid setting the dining table. I hear Lars laughing, and I start to relax. Dinner is ready and smells wonderful; Sean is a great cook, and everyone is hungry. As I give Lars his crutch and my arm for balance, Freyja looks at him and asks, "What's wrong with your leg?" and Lars responds, "I don't have one."

I explain, and Freyja says, "I'm so sorry. I didn't know; Mom never tells me this stuff." I hug Freyja and sit her beside Lars. The meal is so good; we all clean our plates as Yoshi noses around for scraps. "Sorry, no human food for you."

I kiss Lars and help Sean load the dishwasher. The rest of the family is playing a game of *Monopoly* in the living room, and I hear laughter as Lars pulls a Go to Jail card. I watch for a few minutes; Lars looks exhausted. After our long day of travel, I know he needs rest. I give everyone a hug and kiss, and they all do the same for Lars. He is fading fast, so we all agree to meet for breakfast—not too early—and drive back to the hotel. I'm tired, and I know Lars has no energy left. I remove my makeup and hold Lars's cock to pee, smile, and say, "Always a privilege."

We collapse on the king-size bed, and I say, "Yeah, this is what I need for us." We are both asleep in just a few minutes. I wake when the phone rings, remembering our wakeup call. Rested, Lars is now talkative about the family. He likes everyone, especially Freyja. "You were right—your daughter definitely had lots of questions and advice. I told her I think my PTSD is almost gone and how much you have helped me with it." I tell Lars I love him and, "Let's go have breakfast with the family, sans Yoshi." We meet up with them and all enjoy a long, leisurely breakfast of eggs benedict, waffles, and sausage. Sean and Lars talk about Norway and computers while the girls talk about school and my daughter about the patients she has. She manages six group homes for troubled youth—suicides, self-loathing, and other forms of debasement. She pats my hand and says, "We need to talk later. It's Saturday, so the kids want to go for a swim in the community pool. Sean and Lars can huddle in front of the computer, and we will have our talk." I agree, and pulling up to their house, I park behind their Volvo and ask Sean to help me with Lars, as the driveway is steep, and I don't want a fall to mar the sunny day.

We decide to move outdoors in the early afternoon; Sean is barbequing ribs, the girls are off swimming, and Yoshi has his pride of place on the chaise lounge. Sean has built a large, covered patio in sections, all surrounded by uneven stones. Lars and I are walking slowly on the stones, admiring the roses and avocado trees in the yard. Yoshi abruptly barks, racing in front of us after a black cat trailing across the fence. It startles Lars, and his crutch catches on a stone in the path. He leans forward and tries to catch himself but hits the ground hard, taking the weight on his left stump. Sean calls out for help and comes over to help an embarrassed Lars back up. "Hey, you're bleeding, Lars." I ask him to bring over one of the padded patio chairs. He blinks, and I signal Sean quiet; I can feel Lars shudder, and I know a PTSD attack has started. He holds his stumped arm and watches blood run down its length and drip into the stones. Sean brings the chair, sets it down, and twists it until it's level. I sink into the chair and pull Lars into my lap. He is unable to talk, really shaking now. I pull his head to my chest and shield his vision so that he no longer sees the steady stream of blood down his stump.

"Is he okay? Should I call an ambulance?" Sean asks.

"No, he will be fine. Just give us a little space. Would you bring us some gauze and some warm water?"

Just then, my daughter appears with towels and a basin of water. She pulls Sean away and whispers to him. I presume she is telling him that Lars is having a PTSD event, and he looks over at the sad scene of Lars shaking and bleeding while I am desperately trying to pin his head to my chest and shield his vision. Wrapping a roll of gauze around the stump, I see the immediate bloom of red, and I softly tell them to use the towel. I kiss Lars and whisper, "I'm here; you are safe; just take deep breaths. I'm here. You are safe." The shaking continues but doesn't get worse. Lars is still unable to talk and tries again to hold his injured arm. Ten minutes, fifteen minutes go by, and I feel the change in his breathing. Embarrassed, he apologizes for being clumsy.

"Are you okay to stand a little? I want to put you on the chaise and check your arm."

He nods, and Sean and I walk him to the chaise and get him to lie down. I ask for another basin of warm water and an ace bandage and some peroxide, if they have them. I unwrap the towel around his arm and see a large dark bruise forming, along with several angry scrapes and a large cut, probably from a sharp stone. I know Lars is up-to-date on shots, so I gently wash the arm, careful not to let Lars see as blood is still streaming down the arm. The cut is large but not too deep, so he won't need stitches; I'll butterfly it closed when I get the peroxide to ensure it is clean. I pull a clean towel and apply pressure to the edges of the ragged cut. I hold the pressure there as Lars finally opens his eyes. "It happened again. Sorry."

"Nothing to be sorry for, baby. I'm going to put a towel over your eyes so I can put a dressing on your arm. The peroxide will sting but try to relax. I love you, Lars." I return to the arm and lift the pressure from it. The bleeding is slowed but still trickles in rivulets down under his elbow. I saturate the area with peroxide and let it flow freely, dislodging any dirt or residue from the stone. Lars jerks a little but stays silent, and Sean asks if I need anything else. "Yes, I need a few large Band-Aids and another ace bandage." Families with kids usually have well-stocked medicine cabinets, thank goodness. Satisfied the area is clean, I pull the ragged edges together and place two bandages across the cut, putting tension on it to hold it secure until the bleeding is completely done. It may seep a little, which is why I asked for an ace bandage. Rolled gauze would stain red, whereas the ace bandage will hold gauze against the wound but not show a stain. I pull the towel from Lars's head and look into clear, blue eyes. "All done, baby. I'll bring you some Tylenol; do you hurt anywhere else?"

"Just my pride, love."

I grin and kiss his forehead. "Stay still. I'll be right back." I go to the kitchen and retrieve two pain relievers and two glasses of iced tea.

CHAPTER TWENTY-SIX

"Wow, Mom, Lars is a project, isn't he?" I hug my daughter and say, "I wouldn't have it any other way; I love that man."

"Is he okay now?"

"Yes, these attacks drain his energy, but he just needs to rest a little. Warn the girls when they come back not to mention blood."

"Will do, Mom. You are good with him."

"It's Lars; he draws it out of me in so many ways." I return to Lars, and he takes the pain relievers and his iced tea, then turns to me. "I love you, baby; you always know what to do with me."

"No, Lars, I just go with a gut feeling and instinct. You just bring out the best in me. Now, close your eyes and take a little nap before the ribs are done." He closes his eyes, and I ruffle his blond hair. My fragile Viking.

I leave him to nap and go into the house to use the bathroom. Sean is scrolling the TV with a remote and says, "I thought we could relax and watch a move. I can help you get Lars in here." He stops scrolling and says, "*The Vikings*. Kirk Douglas and Tony Curtis. What do you think?"

"Absolutely no, Sean. Remember Tony Curtis gets his hand whacked off in the film?"

"Sorry, Mom. Glad you remembered; I didn't even think about it."

"Good film—just not good for my Viking." I return to Lars after hugging Sean and thanking him for his help. I caress Lars's good arm and check for any staining on the bandage: nice and clean. The girls burst through the back gate, and Freyja rushes over to us. Before I can say anything, she touches the bandage on his stump and says, "Oh, Grandpa, you got hurt."

Lars opens his eyes and smiles at her as she asks, "Is it okay to call you Grandpa?"

Lars softly tells her, "More than okay, little one, I love it." Freyja bends over and kisses his forehead, and I see a tear trickle down his face. "Imagine me, a grandpa. What a family you have, baby."

"Yes, and now you are a big part of it,

Grandpa." Another tear rolls down his cheek, and I kiss it away. Oh, this man, this man. Can a heart overflow with love and explode? Mine is threatening to do so.

We enjoy the rest of the sunny afternoon, and Yoshi jumps up onto Lars's lap. He rubs her tummy, and she licks his face. Sean calls out that the ribs are done, and he has prepared potato salad and fresh melons on the side. Life is good. We just need to stay healthy enough to enjoy it. I won't eat too much potato salad as my gym visits have waned. Freyja disappears after dinner, and her mom reminds her that it is her week to clear the dishes and load the dishwasher. "I will," she calls out. "I just want to get something upstairs." She skips off, and a few minutes later, she comes back and sits cross-legged in front of Lars. She struggles to remove a backpack and finally pulls it in front of her. "I want to show you my rock collection, Grandpa."

"Oh, great, Freyja—tell me about them. Where they come from? Which one is your favorite?"

She pulls a small brown rock and hands it to Lars. "That's my favorite. I know it isn't pretty, but it's from Norway, where you come from, Grandpa." Tears spill from Lars, and he hugs Freyja tightly. "Grandpa, don't cry."

He hugs her tighter and says, "These are happy tears. You are a gift, Freyja, a wonderful gift."

Eliza stands, smirks at her sister, and tells her to go do her chores. "I want to talk to Grandpa Lars."

"Don't touch my rocks! I'll be right back!"

Eliza pulls out her phone and scrolls through until she finds pictures of her boyfriend. "What do you think—isn't he cute? We go to the movies, and I drive because I have a car and he doesn't."

"Yes, Eliza, he is cute, and so are you—a good match. And you have a car? Such wonderful parents. I never had a car, and now I couldn't drive one, anyway," and he lifts his two stumps.

Realization comes to Eliza, and she says, "I'm sorry, Grandpa—I'll have some fun for you."

Lars turns to me and says, "Come here, Grandma, I need a hug."

Eliza rolls her eyes and says, "Ugh, you guys are too old for this."

We both laugh, and Lars says, "What a family, what a family!"

Eliza then says, "Remember, now you are a part of it! I'm going to go relieve Freyja, so she can finish showing her rock collection to you. Can I drive you back to your hotel?"

"No, honey, we have a rental car, and it's a stick shift."

"Okay, I changed my mind. Buckle up, though."

A quick kiss to both of us, and she is already texting on her phone. Yeah, this is quite a family, but it's time to go back to the hotel and spend some time alone with that king-size bed and walk-in shower.

CHAPTER TWENTY-SEVEN

We all hug and kiss one another goodbye, and Sean helps me with Lars on the steep driveway. I ask for a large garbage bag so that Lars can take a shower and not get the bandages wet, and then we're off. He strokes my leg along the way and again tells me he's sorry about the fall.

I tell him, "It was a wonderful visit, Grandpa. Thank you for visiting with the girls. They truly are a gift, and so are you, Lars. Now, let's get you naked."

Back in our room, I tell him to sit on the bed, so I can put the garbage bag around his arm. I tear the ends and secure it; it should keep it dry. Lars tells me he needs to pee, and I have him hold my shoulder since there are no grab bars near the toilet. I hold his hardening cock and then turn the shower on. It being much larger than the one at home, we stay in the warm water after we are clean and just hug each other. I feel his erection growing, so we dry off with the soft towels and go to the big bed. We kiss deeply, and he kisses and sucks my breasts, then says, "I want to be on top."

"Yeah, I want you on top, too; I like your weight on me."

"I can't satisfy you that way, but I do like it."

"Quit worrying; just fuck me hard. I need your passion right now."

He builds and builds, panting, pushing, and pressing me hard to the already-hard mattress—much harder than our memory foam at home.

"Fuck, baby, I'm going to come."

"Give it to me, Lars. Fill me with your passion!" and he jerks and grunts through his release. A perfect end to a wonderful day.

I think since we are already in California, we should drive down the four hours to Stockton and visit my oldest son, James. I call him and tell him Lars and I are coming for a visit and that we'd be there in the late afternoon. I briefly tell him about Lars's condition and that our relationship is very serious.

"Okay, Mom, we'll plan a nice dinner, and we'll see you soon."

"Great, just watch the dogs when we come as Lars is easily knocked over."

Hours later, we pull into the drive, and I honk the horn. James comes out, smiles, and gives me a hug and a kiss. I haven't seen him in over two years as we are both always working. I help Lars out of the car and give him his crutch. James pats his shoulder and tells Lars, "Great to meet you. Let's go inside and then I'll give you a tour. And don't worry, Mom—the dogs are outside in the enclosed kennel area."

We go inside, and I first take Lars to use the bathroom. He automatically puts his hand on my shoulder for support and looks down, waiting for me to hold his cock. I comply with his silent desire, and we go sit in the living room. In the living room, James tells us his wife, Danay, won't be home until five, and the boys would be home around four, so James tells about his little farm.

"Sheep, chickens, dogs, and raccoons that raid the chicken coop's eggs. The sheep substitute for a lawn mower."

We go out to see the dogs, and I ask, "Stay close, James. Rough terrain is hard with a crutch and balance issues."

Lars says, "Yeah, I took a fall yesterday at your sister's," and holds up his bandaged stump.

"We will be careful—I promise, Mom." The dogs are all barking at the fence line, and James warns Lars that they are basically guard dogs and to watch his hands. Lars smiles and holds up the single right hand as James says, "Sorry, it's an automatic warning for me to give."

Lars, still smiling, asks, "Can I pet some sheep? I want to feel their fur, which I haven't done since I was a boy in Norway."

James says, "Sure, I'll lead a few over here. They'll know that the dogs are penned and follow me." In minutes, several large sheep in full wool follow James across the field, grazing for grass as they move along. Several chickens are now clucking, and many of them have quite beautiful coloring. James names the different breeds, each egg color unique to the breed.

"That's quite an unusual coop," Lars observes.

"I built it," James proudly says. "Now, my unfinished pride and joy is right there in the big garage." He leads us over and remotely opens the huge heavy door, revealing a wall lined with work surfaces, tires, gas cans, and tool chests. The center of the garage holds his twenty-five-year project: a 1967 Mustang Fastback, the rear fender walls altered to accommodate the oversize tires. I have seen it in many unfinished states over the years; now it is pristine, glossy black, and worthy of its Mustang name as he gets in, turns the key, and a loud, throaty roar emanates from the car.

"Fabulous!" Lars exclaims. "Let me sit in it, and you can tell me what you have in it!"

"Recarro seats, really low to the floor. It might be hard to get out of," James warns.

Lars opens a door, looks in, and says, "Yeah, I wouldn't be able to get out. But I do need to sit down—can we go into the house, and you can tell me about the car while you make dinner?"

"Sure! We will find a comfortable chair for you, and you can rest."

"Thank you, I need it."

In the house, James pulls around a chair to face the kitchen and starts to tell Lars all about the jet engine, special transmission, carburetor, shifters, and a host of other details he is proud of. Lars asks specific questions when he seems to know about the car's parts. Waiting for dinner, James brings over some cheese and grapes to take the edge off since we have not had lunch. I'd really like to stay later, but I don't want to tax Lars since it's been a lot of travel lately, strange for one who has been in a VA hospital for years.

Taking me aside, James whispers, "He loves you, Mom; I can tell by his looking at you all of the time. And I can see that you love him too."

Two of the boys, Jacob and Andrew, arrive; Lance can't get away from work. The boys meet Lars and are soon discussing the merits of WWE wrestling; Lars has seen many matches at the VA, a diversion with roommates. Dinner is ready—James has made tacos, refried beans, and homemade tortillas. Lars loves Mexican food, maybe with a little less heat, but the food is still good. A cold Miller Lite means we can indulge in a little more heat.

"Do you have any more of my pain meds with you, baby?"

"Sure, I do. I'll get you two. Rough couple of days, huh?"

After dinner, we start getting ready to leave, and I take him to pee since the drive is long, and he is tired. Just as we come out of the house, Danay, James's wife, pulls into the drive. A round of hellos and goodbyes, hugs and kisses, and promises to come visit us next time. "Yeah, Mom, I know. I've been lax." He hugs Lars. "I'm so glad Mom met you; you are a great guy." In the car, we are only twenty minutes outside of Stockton when Lars falls asleep, though he is restless and rubs his arm. I stop before we get to the hotel. Lars wakes, and I tell him I want to change his bandage and check the wound, but I need some supplies. He tells me it itches and feels hot. Telling him I won't be long, I quickly push a cart around the store, grabbing ace bandages, gauze, betadine, and more Tylenol.

Once we are back in our room, I have him shower without the bandage on. First, I tell him to lie on the bed and turn away from me. I unwrap his ace bandage and am glad he cannot see the bloody gauze stuck to his arm; the wound has been seeping and needs to be cleaned. Dark bruises and angry scrapes, and the wound is hot, like Lars mentioned. I go and get a washcloth, towels, and antibacterial soap from the bath. Keeping Lars still, I gently blot the arm, dry it, and apply some betadine and fresh Band-Aids over the cut, which begins to bleed a bit. I make a thick pad of gauze and then wrap the ace around his arm. "Sorry, I don't want you to shower, so I'll give you a bed bath." I need to see if I have any antibiotics with his medications, and luckily find some penicillin. I think he may have a mild infection starting in the arm, since he is a little warm. No thermometer to check, but with a little penicillin and a few Tylenol, he should be comfortable. "I'll be right back; I need to see if I can get a pan at the front desk, so I can give you a bed bath."

"Okay, baby, don't be long."

The clerk at the front desk takes just a minute to look and returns with a stainless mixing bowl. I thank him, grateful for the help and the clean towels they left when they turned the room. I fill the bowl with hot, soapy water, grab some washcloths and towels, and return to my sleepy Viking. He has rolled onto his back, so I clean his face and neck, rinse and wipe under his arms and chest, ruffling the curly, blond hair. I continue down and carefully clean his belly and genitals and a quick run over his backside. I change the water and return to clean his legs and feet. He is shivering, so I put the bowl and dirty washcloths in the bath. I cover him and roll him to his side, so I can spoon with him. "Sleep, baby, sleep."

He is already sleeping as I play with his curly pubic hair. I kiss his shoulder, clean up the bath a bit, strip, and take a hot shower. I put on clean sweats and enjoy the few minutes of alone time. I call my daughter and ask if they could come to the hotel for breakfast before our 11:00 a.m. flight. "Lars is a bit under the weather."

She asks if she can bring the girls, and I say, "I would be sad if you didn't, and Grandpa Lars would be disappointed."

I wake Lars the next morning at 7:30, get him dressed, and give him more medications. He is groggy but anxious to see the girls. At breakfast, we have hot tea and pancakes, fierce hugs and kisses, and Freyja waves, "Goodbye, Grandpa Lars! Come back soon!"

"I don't want to leave, but I don't feel well."

We go back to the room. Everything is all packed, and I tell Lars to pee here because I can't go to the restroom with him at the airport. I get Lars into the car and return to the room to get our bags. I drive to the rental car agency and they take us to the airport in a shuttle van. A short wait through security, and we are at the gate a few minutes before first call. Four hours and we will be home. We both sleep on the flight home. It will be a while before we travel again; it is just too tiring for both of us.

CHAPTER TWENTY-EIGHT

Once home, I drop the bags in the studio, and we both collapse in the bed, sleeping until 6:00 p.m. Lars asks for Tylenol, and I take his temperature—101 degrees. I tease him to lighten the mood. "I'm not sure if this thermometer is working. I should really use the old-fashioned kind and put it in your ass." He frowns and says, "No way."

We have a tuna sandwich and clam chowder. I need to go to the grocery store in the morning and do laundry. I wonder if we could afford a maid; my seventy years are catching up to me. Lars is five years younger than me, but with his limitations, we are about equal. I call Dr. Cross in the morning and tell him I won't make my group. "Lars is a little sick." I relay the happenings from our trip, and he says to double the penicillin, keep up the

Tylenol, and do anything I can to avoid blood. "I am going to order a new anxiety script; I have seen the litany of research, and it is positive with PTSD patients."

"Great, I'll let Lars know. Thanks, Dr. Cross, and tell the guys I'm sorry, but I will see them next week." I make some warm tea, collect the meds, give Lars a kiss, and tell him about the conversation with Dr. Cross. I'll go down and pick up that prescription later today at the VA; no charge for vets. We both squeeze into our small shower in our home, his bandage off. Then I join him in bed. "How about a massage? I want to touch you everywhere."

"Magic hands, magic feelings."

I gather the supplies I need to clean and rebandage his arm. It looks better than yesterday, and I feel no heat, though there's still a little swelling. I grab some massage oil and nuke it for thirty seconds. "Nice and warm. Roll onto your back, Lars."

He smiles and says, "I'm going to like this."

"Yes, you are." I know he is feeling better when I knead and prod his muscles, and he pulls my hand down to his cock. "Knead this muscle." He is already growing and flexing his hips. I grip him tightly as the oil smooths the friction and promotes groans from Lars. He rolls toward me and scrapes some oil from his chest and transfers it to my sex, a little massage for me, and I roll on top of him. "Feel good, baby?" he says.

"I'm feeling great, and I want you to make me come big."

"I have missed having you on top of me, and I want to squeeze your ass."

"Yeah, pull me to you, and I will ride the horse till it crosses the finish line."

"So romantic, baby," and he gently slaps my ass. I am sliding on him and grinding down to feel his length, and he groans and climaxes. "I love you and how much you take care of me," he says, "even though I am a pain in the ass sometimes."

"Yeah, I'm an old lady but one with infinite patience for the man I love." I get up and bring a towel over to remove some oil from both of us.

CHAPTER TWENTY-NINE

"I'm not done with you yet; we missed a few sessions." We talk about our trip and how much he cares for Freyja. He says, "I want to get some special rocks for her and send her a little letter. No typed letter—hand-written—you can help me with it."

"Grandpa, you are already spoiling the grandkids."

"As you know, baby, I always wanted kids, and now we are too old to have them, so I'm most happy to have yours. Treasures to be spoiled."

I kiss him, and he raises his hips again, asking, "I wonder if other grandmas have sex like you do."

"I hope so. I know mine didn't!"

He rises, using his right arm for support, and covers me, the weight now a comforting blanket. We make gentle love and drift to sleep. I wake and ask Lars how he is feeling, and he says, "Good! Back to normal."

I grab the keys as he asks where I'm going, and I explain that I am going to the VA to pick up his new script and that I need his ID. He directs me to his sweatpants pocket. I kiss him and say, "Don't try anything while I'm not here." The VA is busy, and a long line stands in front of the pharmacy window. Forty-five minutes later, I stop and order two lattes, anxious to get home. Lars is not in the bedroom but calls from the library. He is one-finger typing a letter to Freyja, and he says, "I tried to write it, but the paper moves too much." I kiss him, tell him that I brought him a latte, and he finishes the letter.

"Little one, you were a surprise to me, blond and blue-eyed like me. Smart, kind, and I melted when you called me Grandpa. I never thought I would hear that. Thank you, Freyja. Love, Grandpa Lars."

"You are so good, Lars; so glad you love the kids." I look at his new script: okay to take without food. "Take this, a new antianxiety script from Dr. Cross; he is excited at the promising results."

"Oh, baby, you are the best medicine for me."

I pull a notecard and write the letter for Lars, then have him sign it. His signature is shaky and rough, but it's not like the letter is a formal document. I reread the note and kiss him again. "Grandpa Lars," he says. "Yeah, I like it. I never thought it would happen, either."

Lars is in a good mood all day. Whether it's the new pills or just feeling much better, I'll take either one. He is amorous and playfully smacks my ass as I go through the day—laundry, sheet change, bandage change, and the kitchen floor needs a mop. He sits on my office chair in the library and looks through the Blu-rays and DVDs. He pulls several and asks if we can watch a movie.

"Of course—which one do you want to see?" He hands me *The Vikings*. I frown, and he says, "I have never seen it; isn't it any good?"

"Yes, it's a good movie; however, there is a scene in the movie that may trigger an attack. Tony Curtis has his hand chopped off by an English king."

He winces but says, "I think I will be all right. Is it in color?"

"I don't remember, but I think it is." I explain the storyline between Kirk Douglas and

Tony Curtis, the frequent references to Odin, Thor, and other Viking legends, and of course the woman, Morgana, who is promised to an English king but desired by a Viking. "I should tell you: Sean wanted to play this exact movie for you when we were there, but I said no because of the hand incident. You must tell me, Lars, if you start feeling an attack coming on."

"Baby, you know I can't talk during an attack, but I know you can handle it if I do."

"Okay. I love you, Lars. Come, I'll start the movie. We'll have hot turkey sandwiches for an early dinner, and we've got nice, fresh sheets for later."

"I wonder if I'll live long enough to be a great-grandfather," he says as he picks up Freyja's note. I smile and tell him, "You already are. Faith is a real charmer, just two, and blond and blue-eyed like her grandfather Tony. They live just a few hours away, so we can go for a visit soon."

He smiles as he says, "You are too good-looking to be a great-grandmother."

"Oh, you've seen me in the morning when I look my age."

"Your spirit blurs the lines and wrinkles, always beautiful to me. Odin awaits," and he kisses me. He is animated throughout the film and thinks Kirk and Tony are good actors, though Tony Curtis is too pretty for a Viking—and no beard.

"You don't have a beard either, Lars, and I'm glad you don't as I'm not that fond of them."

He rolls his eyes skyward. "I couldn't stand it if I cut myself with a razor."

"Yeah, makes sense, and I don't mind the soft peach fuzz you have," and I tickle his cheek.

"Quit! I want to watch the movie."

The worrisome scene is coming up soon, so I snuggle close, ready for a reaction. I tense when I know the hand will be cut off, but Lars just winces and says, "Glad mine wasn't like that," knowing what was coming. It has got to be the new medication since just a faint wince was his only reaction.

Later, I say, "I have the PTSD group tomorrow—do you want to go with me? You just can't kiss me!"

"Yeah, I would like to see some friends while you see the guys. Okay!"

At the group, Bill is quiet but then jumps up and says, "Arlene! My wife is here!" Remarried now, he is a happy guy. Mike shows me his new driver's license with a commercial endorsement, another happy guy. Then Ryan extends his phone. "Arlene! Look at my girl-friend. She was a nurse and bought it when the field hospital took a hit. She is missing a leg and has a large scar down the right side of her face. Her name is Ann."

"Oh, Ryan, I am so happy for you." Another happy guy.

I see Dr. Cross and ask, "What did you do, order a six-month supply all in one lot?" and he chuckles.

"You know we always have sample packs to try, and they are all on it. How is Lars?"

I tell him about watching *The Vikings* and how there was virtually no reaction. He smiles. "I think we have a winner."

"I think so too. It is like winning a top prize in the lottery." Though I know I really won the top prize with Lars, and I will spend it careful-ly. I love that man so much. "He is still broken but loves me, and he is a new grandpa and great-grandpa, already proud of his family."

"Arlene, you are a wonder."

"Thank you, Dr. Cross. Now I'll go collect Lars and head home with my man."

You know, I used to disagree with the mission statement out in front of the VA: The Cost of Freedom Can Be Seen Here. Yes, it can, in the hearts and souls of the men and women here—not in their physical losses, but their emotional ones. I love these brave souls, and I will always reach out to touch their lives.

I look up and see Lars waiting for me, crutch under his arm and a huge smile. "Come, I'm ready to go home!"

www.ingramcontent.com/pod-product-compliance
Lightning Source LLC
Chambersburg PA
CBHW051345020726
47501CB00007B/2287